Too Dead To Dance

Diane Morlan

Cozy Cat Press   Aurora, IL

Too Dead To Dance © 2010 by Diane Morlan.

All rights reserved. No part of this book may be used or reproduced in any manner whatsoever, including Internet usage, without written permission from Cozy Cat Press except in the case of brief quotations embodied in critical articles and reviews.

First Edition

First Printing 2010

Cover design and illustration by Scott Saunders/ Design 7 Studio, ww.design7studio.com

Published by Cozy Cat Press, cozycatpress@aol.com, website: www.cozycatpress.com

COZY CAT
PRESS

LCCN: 2010923092

Printed in the United State of America

Crochet pattern by Maggie Weldon / Maggie's Crochet http://www.maggiecrochet.com/

This book is a work of fiction. Names, characters, places, and incidents are the product of the author's imagination or are used fictitiously. Any resemblance to actual persons, living or dead, business establishments, events, or locals is entirely coincidental. The publisher does not have any control over and does not assume any responsibility for author or third party websites.

Library of Congress Cataloging-in-Publication Date

Morlan, Diane, 1943—,
Too Dead To Dance / Diane Morlan. — 1st ed.

ISBN: 978-1479395248

PUBLISHER'S NOTE: The recipe contained in this book is to be followed exactly as written. The publisher is not responsible for your specific health or allergy needs that may require medical supervision. The publisher is not responsible for any adverse reactions to the recipe contained in this book.

Dedicated to the Memory of my good friend,

Marie Fournier Julian

January 4, 1945 - November 30, 1985

She always believed in me and encouraged me

to pursue my dreams. We miss you.

Acknowledgements

Writing this book has been one of my greatest adventures. I could not have completed it without the help of my family and friends.

Heartfelt thanks to my daughter, Shirlee Morlan, who taught me about roasting coffee, my grandson, Steven Morlan, my son, Jim Morlan and my daughter-in-law, Eileen Morlan who gave me the confidence to undertake this endeavor and always believed in me.

Thank you Maureen Kelley, Ann-Marie Eggleston and all my co-workers at the Kishwaukee College Library who supported and encouraged me, especially Deb MacManus, Carol Wubbena and DeeAnn Leuzinger my wonderful first readers.

Thanks to my friends Jennifer Walker, for lending me her name, Sheila Weigel whose initial suggestions helped me get started in the right direction, and Patty Herzog, for taking me to my first German folk music festival.

Thank you, Patricia Rockwell, for finding me and taking me on this incredible journey. It would not have happened without you.

Please visit my website, www.DianeMorlan.com, for news and information on Jennifer Penny mysteries. Become a Facebook fan of Diane Morlan, Author.

Diane Morlan

1

Friday

The first time I met the butcher he almost ran over me. He didn't chase me down the road or anything. In fact, the whole thing was mostly my fault.

I was hurrying from the parking lot because I thought I was late. I hate being late but my stupid garage door opener decided not to work today. I had to drag open the door by hand and it had taken enough time to get me off schedule. I carried a box filled with one- pound bags of coffee beans that I had roasted just last night.

As I crossed the dirt road that runs through the Maron County fairgrounds, I twisted my foot in a notorious Minnesota gopher hole, did a pirouette, and fell on my fanny in the middle of the road. Down I plopped, while the box flew out of my hands. Gold and black sacks rained down on me.

Looking to my left, I saw a red cargo van bearing down on me. It was so close that the only action I could take was to throw my arms over my head and lean forward into my knees.

I heard the van screech to a halt. I peeked out to my left and saw the bumper of the truck about three feet from my head.

A tall, sandy-haired man dressed all in white jumped out and helped me to my feet.

"Are you okay?" He asked, helping me to my feet.
"I think so." My ankle was beginning to throb.
"For God's sake, Honey! I almost ran over you."
"Why were you speeding? This is a fairground, not a race track!"

"Gee, I wasn't going that fast, Sweetie," he said while helping me to my feet.

"Thanks," I replied automatically, brushing the back of my white slacks. They felt damp from the morning dew. I leaned down and began picking up coffee bags. "Let's blame the stupid gopher who decided to make a home next to a road."

"Let me help you," he said picking up bags of coffee and stuffing them into the box. One bag had split and coffee beans spilled onto the ground. I carefully lifted it and set it in the box. I'd take it home for my personal use. Two bags were crushed but the beans were safe. I'd use those to brew coffee for tasting samples today. When the box was full, the man lifted it and held it out to me. Our hands touched. His hand was unusually cold on this hot summer morning.

"I can carry this for you. Where are you headed?" he asked, circling his arm around me and touching my waist.

Grabbing the box, I twisted around so I was facing him. "No problem. Thanks for the help. I can handle it from here."

"You sure? I don't mind. I did almost run over you." Backing away, I smiled which probably looked more like a grimace, flustered at the way he was grinning at me. I turned and hurried away, calling over my shoulder, "No problem. Thanks."

I heard the truck door slam shut and turned to make sure he was leaving. He waved at me through the window over the sign painted on the door; *Metzger's Meat Market, Hermann, MN*, then gunned the engine and zoomed through the gate I had just entered.

Peeking into my purse, I was relieved that the small white bakery bag holding a single chocolate covered donut still lay tucked inside. My nutritionally poor but tasty breakfast. I'd have to make another trip to my car in order to get all the coffee I had roasted to sell today at the Polka Daze Festival. There must be a better way to haul my coffee to the booths at these craft shows but a little red wagon wouldn't fit in my Civic. I put the problem on my mental "to do" list.

I struggled up to the door of the Home Arts Building and grabbed the door handle. I pulled the handle toward me and nearly yanked my arm out of the socket. Locked. Guess I wasn't late after all. During the Maron County Fair, needlework and home baked goods filled this long narrow building to the rafters. Now at Polka Daze, various crafters and small business owners rent space and set up booths to sell their wares. I rattled the door hoping I could shake it open and jumped when someone behind me said, "Let me open that for you."

A distinguished looking man with silver grey hair wearing baggy jeans and a plaid shirt hurried up to the door and stuck a key in the lock. "Mornin'. Saw you talking to my brother, Al. You okay?"

"I'm fine," I said, looking at my watch. It read 7:55. "I was afraid I'd be late."

"Nope. You're the first one here." He reached inside the door and flipped the light switches. The lights made the building less ominous, but without people, it still echoed with each step I took.

"I'll come back later for a cup of coffee," the man called out to me.

When I looked back, he gave me a short, two-finger salute, then turned and walked away. Only then did I realize that he was the Fest Meister. I had met him last night when he presided over the nightly keg tapping. I hadn't recognized him without his lederhosen.

Thinking about the man's silver grey hair as I entered the cool, dimly lit Home Arts building, I wondered if my hair would look that good if I quit coloring it. I hadn't seen my real hair color since my fortieth birthday, six years ago. I had decided I didn't want to be a little old grey haired lady, so I found a great beautician. Now I wear my light brown hair in a short sassy bob.

I hurried toward my booth, anxious to set down the heavy box of coffee. I dropped the cumbersome box onto the front table of my booth and I pulled the bakery bag out of my purse.

My first chore was to make coffee for the fest-goers to sample as well as a cup to go along with my yummy donut. The black table cover hung unevenly across the table situated along the side of my booth that held my DeLonghi coffee maker. I try to position the tables in my booth so I don't have my back to my customers while I pour them a sample cup of coffee.

I tugged the tablecloth back in place and then centered the coffee pot. My part-time helpers must have been in a hurry to leave last night. Besides the cockeyed cloth, the table itself was askew, one side pushed up against the table in the next booth.

Still holding onto the donut bag, I reached under the table for the gallon jug of spring water I use to fill the coffee pot. My foot slipped. Looking down I saw a puddle at my feet. My eyes traveled to the edge of the gooey mess under my right foot. I screamed.

A body lay on the floor partly under the side table of my stand. I threw up my arms and the donut bag went flying across the booth.

Long legs encased in lederhosen, the man lay in a pool of reddish-black substance, which I figured was blood. His face was turned toward the wall. I spun around and slowly walked toward the exit. I wanted to run but could barely move. Digging in my purse, I pulled out my cell phone and with shaky fingers called 9-1-1.

I told the police dispatcher someone lay dead in the Home Arts Building at the Fest Grounds. I must have been blubbering because she made me repeat myself several times.

"Can you describe what you see, please?"

I stopped walking, turned to look back at my booth, and said between clenched teeth, "Lady, I see a dead man in a puddle of bloody goo. I stepped in it. What more do you need to know?"

"Are you sure he's dead and not just passed out?"

I stomped my foot. "He's sort of grey, his mouth is open, and his eyes are, too. He sure looks dead to me."

"Did you say Fest Grounds? That's outside the city limits. I'll contact the Sheriff's Department. Leave the building immediately and wait outside for the sheriff. And don't touch anything else," she ordered.

I barked at her, "I watch CSI. I know that. Besides, I sure don't want to be in here any longer."

I looked around, suddenly realizing that I was alone in this place with a corpse. I fled through the exit door, almost knocking down the guy who had unlocked the door for me.

"What's wrong? Why were you yelling? Are you okay? You look like you saw a ghost."

"I think I did. There's a dead man in there." Without warning, my eyes began to tear up and I found myself crying. Although I was sure I didn't know who the dead person was, I was filled with dismay. The only dead bodies I had ever seen were at funerals. Those people lay on white silk not on a cold cement floor surrounded in blood.

I felt a hand on my elbow guiding me to a park bench just outside of the door. I tried to smile at the Fest Meister and thank him. While we sat on a bench outside the building's door waiting for the deputies to arrive, the man introduced himself to me.

"I'm Frank Metzger. When I'm not the Fest Meister, I'm at Metzger's Meat Market over on the highway. My brother, Al, and I own the place. This is how I spend my vacation every year. Are you going to be all right?"

"I'll be okay. My name is Jennifer Penny. I'm just

Too Dead to Dance

shook up. It was quite chilling."

An ambulance with lights whirling and siren screaming pulled up in front of the building. Two young men got out and asked us where to find the sick person.

"The man isn't sick, he's dead."

"We'll make that decision, Miss. Show me where he is, please," said the tallest Emergency Medical Technician.

Shaking my head and pointing I said, "He's in there. The dispatcher told me to stay out and I plan to do exactly what she said."

The EMT's entered the building and I listened to hear what was going on in there. It was very quiet.

After the Emergency Medical Technicians had been inside for a few minutes, the shorter EMT came through the door, cell phone to his ear. "No, Sir, we didn't touch anything. Just checked his pulse, and then got out of there. Yes, Sir, I understand."

He flipped the phone shut and stuck his head in the door. "Stan, get out of there, the cops are on their way."

A few minutes later, the taller EMT swaggered out of the building, slapping his hands together just as a squad car sped into the fairgrounds, lights whirling. It came to a grinding halt two feet from where we sat.

2

A large black man in a cheap rumpled suit heaved himself out of the passenger side of the car. I stood up as he ambled toward me. "Mrs. Heinz, don't tell me you're the one who found this body?"

I had met Lieutenant Delmar Jacobs a few months ago when I had a break-in at my coffee warehouse. "I'm afraid so. And it's terrible. I wish I didn't have that picture in my head, but please call me Jennifer. It's not Heinz anymore, either. I took back my maiden name, Penny."

"Okay, Ms. Penny. Can you wait here while we check this out?"

I heard a car door slam and glanced over to the driver's side of the squad car. A gorgeous dark haired man with a compact body strode toward us. I could see that, although not more than 5'9", his solid build gave him a look of formidability. He looked down at me. I'm short. Everyone looks down at me.

"Detective Jerry Decker," he said sticking out his hand to shake mine. When I grasped his hand, a little shock went through mine. He felt it too, I thought.

"So, you knew the victim, Ma'am?"

Ma'am? I thought. Did he say Ma'am? Did I look like a Ma'am? I looked him right in the eye, ready to tell him off. His eyes were light brown, like coffee diluted with cream. When I got a whiff of his musky aftershave, my knees went weak and I almost fell.

"Are you okay, Ms. Penny?" Lieutenant Jacobs grabbed my arm. "Maybe you should sit down."

"No, no. I'm fine." I straightened up and took a deep breath. I moved around until my back was to the building so neither man could see my damp posterior. "I don't know who that man in there is. I've never seen him before."

Detective Decker, the aromatic cop, looked at me with a tiny smile pulling at the sides of his mouth. "You touch anything in there?"

I started to say something snotty to him but when I looked up at him my knees waffled again. What the hell was going on here? How could this sexy man have such an effect on me? It must have been purely physical because I didn't even know him.

I had been married for more than twenty years. I didn't know how to interact with a man at this level. And I wasn't sure I wanted to. It was probably just the shock of seeing a dead man that had my emotions all messed up.

Lieutenant Jacobs took my arm and helped me back to the park bench. "You sit here while Detective Decker and I go take a look. Jerry, call the State boys and get their Forensics Team out here."

Jacobs looked at me and said, "Who has the booth Detective Decker whipped his cell phone out of a leather case hooked to his belt like an old western sheriff drawing his gun. He snapped open the phone and hit a speed dial number. Before he turned away, he winked at me. Winked at me!

I started to tell him off when my stomach did a flip and a gurgle. "Oh," I whispered to my stomach and knees "stop that. I don't think I'm ready for this."

Vendors began to arrive to open their booths. When a group of them gathered at the entrance started mumbling about the delay, Lieutenant Jacobs came out of the building.

Raising both hands for quiet, he said, "There's been an incident. This building will be closed for the day. It'll reopen tomorrow, if we're finished."

Jacobs looked at me and said, "Who has the booth next to yours? The one closest to the door."

"That lady wearing the blue dirndl." I pointed out a stout fortyish lady in the group of vendors. I had met her yesterday, the first day of the festival. "Her name is Trudy."

"Thanks, Ms. Penny. Sit tight. I'll be back to talk to you in a little while."

Jacobs went over and talked quietly to Trudy. He escorted her into the building, his huge ebony hand gently touching her back. In a few seconds, we heard a shriek.

More deputies arrived and two of them wound the yellow crime scene tape around a large tree and brought it across the broad doors, anchoring it to a drainpipe at the corner of the building.

I sat there waiting for Lieutenant Jacobs to return, really just wanting to get out of there. The sun beat down on me and I began to perspire. I shifted to the other end of the bench to be in the shade and noticed red on my new sneakers. Darn! I saw that I had left little red footprints like ink from a rubber stamp marching down the sidewalk. I had just taken the new sneakers out of the box this morning. I wondered what it would take to get the blood off the shoe. Probably more than Tide.

When the county coroner arrived, he pompously traipsed up the sidewalk to the building while his old black bag bumped against his leg.

At the last election, the coroner-slash- dentist had run uncontested. After his reelection, people had joked that only his family had voted for him. The people I know swore they had left that choice blank. Mickey Mouse got two write-in votes.

Amongst all the activity going on, Trudy shuffled out of the exhibit hall and sat down next to me.

"The dead guy is Wes, the trumpet player in my husband Ray's band," she whispered to me. "I identified him."

"Oh my God!" I whispered to Trudy, "That's the guy Sister Bernadine had the fight with yesterday." "That's right. I heard your friend telling you about it. He only recently started to play in Ray's band. I only knew him from his reputation. Ach, *Gott in himmel,* I need to call Ray. I think Wes was a bit of a scoundrel. I know he was in a lot of trouble when he was a kid. But he didn't deserve to die. Oh, this is terrible for the band."

Frank Metzger, leaning against a sturdy oak tree next to the park bench took the toothpick out of his mouth. "Isn't going to be too good for Polka Daze either. It's our biggest tourist event and brings a lot of money into Hermann. This could hurt attendance."

I handed Trudy a tissue to wipe her eyes. "It'll be okay, you guys. Lieutenant Jacobs is a good cop. He'll find out who did this."

The two detectives finally came out of the building and walked over to Trudy and me. Detective Decker took out a small notebook and said, "Ladies, I need you to give me the names of people who knew the deceased." "Well, let's see," Trudy answered. "Besides my husband, Ray, there's the other guys in the band. Clara Schmidt, our drummer and her husband, Vic. He plays the clarinet. Then there's Bobby Reinhart. He plays the euphonium."

"What the heck is that?" asked Detective Decker.

"A euphonium? It's a small tuba. Don't know much about music, do ya?" Trudy shot back.

Detective Decker sat down next to Trudy. As she mentioned names, he jotted them down in his pocket-sized notebook.

I sat there trying to look nonchalant. After all, I didn't actually see anything. What other people had told me didn't count. Isn't that hearsay? If I didn't say anything then I wouldn't be lying, but Jacobs was too smart to let me get away with that.

"What do you know about this, Ms. Penny?"

"Nothing. I never saw that man before I almost fell over him. And please call me Jennifer."

"Okay, Jennifer, talk to me. I heard a friend of yours had a fight with this guy yesterday."

Where the heck had he heard that? He just got here. I looked at Trudy and she looked away, her neck and face turning pink, then red.

Standing, I touched my index finger to my lips, looking around as if to be thinking. "You must mean Sister Bernadine. I heard she had a little tiff with this Wes guy yesterday, but it was nothing."

"Where can I find her?"

When Jacobs stared at me with eyes as dark as espresso, I caved. Still trying to keep from telling him anything I said, "Gee, she could be anywhere. She works at the church and she volunteers at the battered women's shelter. She has a sister in Mankato somewhere. I don't really know." I smiled up at him through my bangs, trying to look innocent.

"Jennifer, give me her phone number. Stop being difficult."

"Okay, but please let me call her." I didn't want a cop to break the news to her. I opened my cell phone and pressed her speed dial number.

When the call went to voice mail I said, "Bernie, you need to come over to the fairgrounds. There's a problem at the Home Arts building. Come over as soon as possible. It's important." I hung up.

"She didn't have anything to do with this, you know." I gave Jacobs one of my sweetest smiles. He snorted and shook his head. He pointed to the park bench and said, "Sit."

As I sat down, I noticed Detective Decker with Trudy, talking to the other musicians in Trudy's husband's band. I hoped Decker hadn't seen my dewy rear. I wondered if I could sit here until he left. Fat chance of that

Turning my head, I looked up at Lieutenant Jacobs and said. "I gave Sister Bernadine a ride home last night so she wasn't even around here. Besides, she'd never do anything to hurt another person. For heaven's sake, she's a nun!"

"Did you two come here together last night?" He asked, sitting next to me.

"No, I ran into her after I left my coffee booth."
"Why did you need to give her a ride? How did she get here to begin with?"

Darn, I thought, this is one smart man. He handed me a sweaty bottle of water. I rolled it across my forehead and then twisted off the cap and took a long pull from the much-appreciated water.

"Okay, Jennifer, tell me everything. Let's start at the beginning. What happened here yesterday?"

I took a deep breath and began to tell him about yesterday's events.

3

Thursday

When Natalie Younger had strolled into the Home Arts Building with her little white clutch purse tucked under her arm, my first thought was to hide under the table. The woman drove me nuts. The fastest phone in the Midwest, she never heard a piece of gossip she didn't hurry to pass on.

My coffee booth at the Polka Daze Festival sat in the prime location, across from the wide double doors. Most people, like Natalie, turned right and circled the perimeter. They checked out the crafts and merchandise for sale, then ended up at my booth near the end of the circuit.

Today you could buy handmade earrings, hand-blown glass figurines, and hand-painted and shellacked little wooden boxes. A crowd of on-lookers stood in front of a booth watching as a lady demonstrated how to make tiny dumplings called spaetzle.

A plump lady making lace in the booth next to mine called over to me. "Did you lose something, dear? Why is your head under the table?"

I straightened up while running my hand through my short chestnut hair. When ruffled, it tends to stand up on end. My friends say it makes me look like a frightened porcupine.

In the spirit of Hermann, Minnesota's annual Polka Daze, the woman wore a blue and white dirndl, the traditional German dress. She looked ready to grab bucket and milk a cow.

In contrast to my red "Kiss Me I'm German" t-shirt, her crisp cotton print dress flowed all the way to the floor with a white lace-edged bib hugging her ample bosom. Her hands zipped along, as she flipped wooden bobbins wrapped with white thread, making lace, her head nodding while I explained.

The front table of her booth was a cascade of lace. Doilies, table runners, lacy collars, baby dresses, shawls and wraps, even a tablecloth and a bedspread, all lacy and made of crochet thread, pearl cotton thread and fingerling yarn in a rainbow of colors.

I kept an eye on Natalie's progress toward my booth. "I'm hiding from a lady I just saw. She's a terrible gossip and I know if she stops at my booth, she'll talk my ear off."

"Oh, I see. You're against gossip. Is it a religious thing?"

"Heavens, no! I love gossip. I mean, you know, I like to know what's going on. Isn't that shameful? That Natalie's so negative. She never talks about the good things that happen to people. It's depressing to listen to her for more than a few minutes, but Lord forgive me—I'm easily sucked into a conversation with her. When my marriage went to the dogs, she blathered to everybody in Hermann that I was a terrible wife."

Behind her booth, a sign on the wall proclaimed "Trudy's Lace Haus, Itzig, MN," I hadn't been to the tiny town of Itzig in twenty years. "Is Itzig still the smallest town around here?"

"Ach, yah. Two hundred twelve people. If we were in Europe, it would probably be called a hamlet. We're only eight miles west of Hermann, so we shop here. We think of Hermann as 'the big city,'" she laughed.

I laughed along with her. Hermann's population is under 12,000, not what most people would consider a city of any kind.

While we chatted, Natalie bounced up to my booth. I stood behind my table, now only half filled with Primo Gusto Coffee Roasters bags lined up like dominos. Turning toward her, trying to look business-like, I hoped she hadn't heard me complaining about her.

"Jennifer! What are you doing here? Is business so bad you have to hawk your coffee at a craft fair?"

I looked at her, so perfectly groomed with every hair in place. She was wearing cool green Capri pants and a white top with an appliquéd sailboat on it. Natalie looked as if she'd just finished posing for a Macy's ad.

Unlike me, she had no coffee stains on her blouse nor did she appear rumpled in the heat. How do people like her stay so fresh and crisp? For cripes sake, she was wearing pumps at a fairgrounds! Who does that? I looked down at my soiled sneakers and recognized another reason I couldn't stand her.

"Actually, Natalie," I replied through clenched teeth, "It's a great way for me to expand my customer base. This Columbian coffee is dark and strong. I call it *'Dunkle Starke.'* Would you like a cup?"

"I suppose. Did you hear about Sister Bernadine?" "Sister Bernadine? Did something happen to her? Is she okay?"

"Oh, she's fine, just running off her big mouth again." Natalie said. "She got into a loud fight with one of the musicians in the Windig Sangers Band and the guy called her the 'B' word. Then she said even though he'd always been a less than honest person, she'd continue to pray for him. He got really mad, shook his fist at her, and told her he didn't need her prayers and if she didn't keep her nose out of his business, she'd be sorry. It's a terrible thing to say to a nun, don't you think?"

I gazed at her and shook my head. She sure could

say a lot without taking a breath.

"How do you like this coffee?" I asked, trying to change the subject. I knew the nun's temper and I didn't want to hear anymore. "It's a favorite of the people here at the festival. I just roasted the beans last night."

Natalie took a sip from the paper cup. "This is actually good, Jennifer. I had no idea you knew what you were doing. Although it's way too hot for coffee today." She ran her index finger across one of the coffee bags, and looked at her fingertip. Guess she thought my coffee was dusty. "I'll take a pound of this."

While I put her purchase in a bag and wrote up the receipt, Natalie kept on yakking.

"I think you should talk to Sister Bernadine. That man looked downright mean. She never did know when to keep her nose out of other people's business. Did you hear about Mrs. Reinhart, the high school counselor? Her daughter, Nancy is pregnant. I can't imagine how embarrassing that must be for her. So, is your divorce final yet?"

"Not yet. I'd rather not talk about it, if you don't mind."

"Of course not, I understand. Are you still staying at Megan's? I know she's your best friend but I can't imagine living with her. She's such a smart aleck, it would drive me nuts."

"No, I've moved into a townhouse across the street from her."

"Oh, how nice. I heard that Edwin is seeing a younger woman. Marty something or another. Do you know her?"

"You know, Natalie, I'm kind of busy, can we talk about this another time?"

Natalie looked around to see if there were people behind her waiting. There wasn't another customer in sight. Pursing her lips she said, "That's fine, Jennifer. I suppose it's hard to talk about it. I have to be going anyway. See ya."

She grabbed her coffee, stuck it in a canvas tote

with a slogan stating, "Everyone Loves a German Girl" over a black, red and yellow heart and swept through the double doorway.

I turned toward Trudy, sitting in her bobbin lace booth, shrugged my shoulders, and handed her a cup of coffee.

She took a tentative sip. "My, this is sure good coffee. I'm Trudy Neumann. I couldn't help overhearing your friend. My husband, Ray, is the leader of the band she was talking about. She didn't mention the person the nun had the argument with, did she?"

I thought for a moment, introduced myself, and then said, "I'm sure Natalie didn't know or she'd have made sure to mention it. I'm still amazed she liked my coffee. She's told our friends I have a strange little hobby. If she only knew how much income this 'little hobby' generates!"

"Probably more than my little lace shop. It's in a converted garage and is plum full of threads and needlework supplies."

"I'll drive over and check it out one day soon. Do you have classes?" I asked.

"Yah, Lots of classes. Customers need an excuse to drive over to Itzeg for supplies. I teach the crochet and tatting classes. Also, bobbin lace making like I'm doing here today. My friend, Clara, she teaches needlepoint and counted cross-stitch. We found a Swedish lady to teach hardanger and huck embroidery. We have it all covered except for knitting. I knit some but not enough to teach a class. If you give me your email address, I'll put you on my newsletter list. Well, Clara will put you on the email list. I don't know anything about those computers."

"That sounds good to me," I replied and scribbled my email address on a scrap of paper and handed it to Trudy.

"Ah, my dear," she said. "There's a price tag in your hair."

I ran my hand through my hair again and my fingertips caught on a cellophane sticker. "Guess my hair cost $12.95." I groaned certain Natalie would find my messiness amusing.

"Is this the first year you've had a booth here? I don't remember you from last year," Trudy asked.

"Yes, this is my first year here or at any of the festivals around here. Mostly I've been selling my coffee to restaurants. Recently I started an internet website and I thought these festivals and fairs would be a good way to get more individual customers."

"Oh, there we go again, talking about computers. Sometime I think I live in a different world."

"It's really not so hard to learn, Trudy. They give free classes at the library. You should take one. Then you won't feel so out of touch."

"What a good idea. Maybe I will. Thanks, Jennifer." Trudy and I chatted between customers and browsers. "Ray and I live in Itzeg. We're not on the farm anymore. Ray still farms but the house got too big when the kids moved out, so we moved to town."

"It sounds like music is important to your family." "Oh, yah, Ray's been playing in polka bands forever. In fact, we met at the Itzeg Germanfest, thirty-five years ago. My, the time goes by fast."

"Oh, I remember Germanfest," I said. "Does the festival still bring in more people than the population of Itzeg?"

"Yah, but there's good things about living in a little village. I think our kids were safer there. At least none of them got in any trouble when they were growing up. They loved Ray's music and still reminisce about all the fun they had as kids going to all the gigs with me and Ray."

"I'm sure they have wonderful memories. Are they all grown up now?"

"Yah, and the girls all moved to Minneapolis. The oldest is in a rock band. Not my style but she loves it. I guess Itzeg was too small for them. But my boy,

Charlie, he works the farm with his dad. He lives here in Hermann. I guess boys need their privacy." Trudy brought her finger to her lips and looked up as if she was trying to remember something. "Ya know, I think Sister Bernadine might have been arguing with, the newest member of Ray's band."

"What makes you think that, Trudy?"

"I'm not sure but he's somewhat of a hothead. Before we even set up this morning, I saw him arguing with the Fest Meister. And last weekend the band played at the local Elks Club. Wes blew up at Bobby, another guy in the band, for cutting in on him while he was dancing with this little blonde cutie. They weren't supposed to be on the dance floor anyway, so Ray bawled out both of them."

Trudy laughed. "Turns out the girl was Bobby's sister, Bridget, and he didn't want Wes anywhere near her. Right now Wes is bunked in at his mother's house until he gets it all together, whatever that means."

We were snickering when a slightly balding man with salt and pepper hair and a beer belly protruding over his lederhosen, came up to Trudy's booth and handed her a Styrofoam box.

I was thinking about how silly these men looked with their knobby knees and hairy legs in the short pants. I wondered if the leather pants chaffed.

"Here's your dinner, Honey. Are you sure you don't want to just shut down and go home when the building closes at nine? I can get a ride with Vic and Clara."

"And miss your accordion solo at the nightly closing ceremony? Not on your life!"

He patted her shoulder, and grinned my way. "She's totally devoted to me."

Trudy said, "Jennifer, meet my husband, Ray."

Ray shook my hand. "Nice to meet ya. Has Trudy been talking your ear off?"

"Not at all. She just told me what a great band you have."

Too Dead to Dance

"Yah, she's my biggest fan." We chatted for a few more minutes, and then Ray left to return to the band and their evening performance.

Around the dinner hour only a scattering of customers were strolling through the building. I sold a few more pounds of coffee and Trudy had a flourish of business with some women who spoke broken English until Trudy answered in German. They laughed and chatted in the mother tongue while Trudy tallied up their purchases.

After they left, Trudy turned to me. "Those women were either musicians or spouses with one of the bigger bands. They'll go to several other festivals around the country before going back to Germany."

"I see," I replied. "Perhaps that's why they didn't buy any coffee. It probably wouldn't be very fresh by the end of summer when they return to Germany."

"No, they just want to save their money to buy jeans. They each buy a suitcase full of blue jeans to take back to Germany every year. I guess jeans are very expensive there and all the teenagers want them. They sure didn't mind drinking your samples, did they?"

"Maybe they'll find it so delicious that they'll come back and buy some from me."

"Yah, sure they will." Trudy laughed.

Sally Baumgartner, my most reliable part-time worker, came to relieve me around five o'clock. As usual, she bounced in with a greeting for everyone, ready and able to do whatever I asked of her.

"Hi, Sally. Is that a new vest?" I asked.

"Yes, it's new," she answered. "Do you like it?"

"Of course I do. Where do you get them? They're so attractive and unusual"

"My grandmother was born in the Ukraine. She makes them for me. I used to think they were awful and refused to wear them. Lately I noticed how beautiful and unique they are and got the idea of making them part of my personal style."

"They certainly are unique and this one really looks great with those earrings."

Her chunky wood earrings, dangling almost to her shoulders, were a perfect complement to the brown vest embroidered with bright red and yellow flowers.

"I made the earrings. Do you really like them?"

"I do. I don't know where you find the time to make jewelry with all your activities. You're the busiest girl I know."

Sally blushed, obviously pleased with the compliment. "I guess we just make time for the things that we find important."

"Well, not to put more on your plate but have you ever thought of asking your grandmother to teach you to make those vests? You could sell the vests with matching earrings at festivals like this. It might pay your way through college."

"Wow! I never thought of that. It sounds like a great idea. Do you think people would buy them?"

"Of course. People love new and unusual things, especially in fashion. You should try it."

"Would you help me with getting booths and pricing and all that stuff?"

"I'd be glad to, Sally. Why don't you start by getting some inventory ready? Make some vests with matching earrings. We'll price them separately but display them together and most people will buy both. They do that in stores all the time because most people don't trust their fashion sense and aren't sure what goes with what."

"Wow, that sounds great. How will I know what to charge?"

"Check out what the going price is in a store for earrings and vests that are made in factories. You'll charge more but it will give you a baseline. Then when you make the items keep track of how much you spend. We'll figure the price from that information."

"Jennifer, you're so smart. Thank you."

"No problem. Let me know when you're ready

Too Dead to Dance

and we'll get together to price your items and find the right events for you to sell them at."

I gave Sally some last minute instructions, grabbed my purse, and headed for the door. "I'll see you tomorrow, Trudy. Have a nice evening."

"Oh, I will. Ya' know, even after all these years, I still enjoy listening to Ray's band. I also like to have a beer or two." She began to hum while she swung the bobbins, twisting them around little pins stuck in a pillow.

Tomorrow would be another big day for sales so I needed to have at least fifty pounds of coffee roasted and bagged for the day. And Saturday and Sunday would be even busier days. I made a quick phone call to Mark Jensen, another part-time worker and asked him to be available this weekend to roast coffee or fill in here at the Fest.

I started coffee roasting as a hobby when I lived in Illinois. I'd come across a book in the library and thought I'd try it. The first time I roasted the coffee beans in an old popcorn popper over the stove in my kitchen, Edwin Heinz, my soon-to-be -ex-husband had a fit. Okay, so it did get smoky and the house smelled like coffee for a week, but, hey, I happen to like the smell of coffee.

After that, Edwin reluctantly agreed to allow me to roast the coffee on our patio over a Coleman stove. I hadn't thought about selling it. I just gave it to family and friends as gifts.

It was my friend, Megan who suggested that I try to sell the coffee to area restaurants. She had also set up my internet website.

I was really enjoying working the booth at this festival. There are so many festivals in Minnesota, western South Dakota and northern Iowa that I had chosen only the best ones to attend this year. It had taken some research but so far this summer the four shows I'd worked had been surprisingly profitable and fun. And some customers from previous craft shows had already put in orders through my website.

By far the best part was meeting people face to face. The coffee I sold to restaurants and over the internet didn't allow me to see people enjoying my brew and I didn't get to talk to them personally.

Polka Daze was turning out to be the most profitable of all of them, probably because it runs for four days— Thursday through Sunday, one or two days longer than most other events. And it had a huge turnout. German-Americans from across the Midwest eagerly wait each year for Polka Daze. And Germans love their coffee.

It's also convenient for me, as it's held in the town where I live. I'm able to roast fresh coffee daily instead of trying to estimate how much I need before I leave for a festival. I like to roast beans daily to be certain my coffee is the freshest it can be for my customers at these events.

When I left the exhibit hall, I fully expected to go to Primo Gusto and roast coffee for tomorrow. Best laid plans and all that.

Too Dead to Dance

4

Thursday evening

I strolled toward the parking lot, thinking about my business options. Soon after we moved to Minnesota from the Chicago suburbs six years ago, I continued to give away my coffee to friends and neighbors. When they began calling to put in orders for coffee, I took my business to the next level, contacting local eateries and giving out samples.

Within a few months, I had negotiated contracts with some of the best restaurants in southwestern Minnesota. Soon coffee orders filled my kitchen counter and supplies in boxes ringed the room, leaving no space to cook or eat.

One day Edwin crashed into a box as he entered the kitchen through the attached garage.

"Get this crap out of the house. Now!" he bellowed. "I've had enough. There isn't even room for you to cook a meal. Not that you've cooked anything besides pizza lately."

The next day I started looking for a place to rent. I found a nice space in the Hermann Industrial Park on the west side of town. A building split into four spaces, the one for rent had been a business of some sort. There was a counter inside the door and a small space in the corner to set up an office. I signed a two-year lease and moved everything out within forty-eight hours of Edwin's hissy fit. It was a month before he noticed that I hadn't just quit but had actually moved into a business location.

After that, he mostly ignored the fact that I ran a business. He just kept telling me that he wouldn't be responsible for any debts that I incurred. It was his suggestion that I incorporate the business to keep him out of it completely.

"I don't want to lose my house over some silly hobby of yours," He had complained.

My business took a huge leap when I started selling it on the Internet. My best friend, Megan Murphy developed and now takes care of my web site where customers are able to order coffee over the internet. My Primo Gusto coffee is shipped to homes all across America.

It was quite a chore to get the website set up. Megan had the know-how, but she wanted it to be a relaxed easy to use site. I agreed with the easy to use part but I wanted it to look professional. I didn't think that pictures of Chippendale models would attract the kind of customers I was looking for.

We finally came to an agreement. The site wouldn't have any half-naked men on it but it would be casual and give the feel of a small coffee shop. Megan worked magic by using backgrounds and helping me with names for the different blends of coffee. We both wanted to get away from the look of a franchise. The result was a cozy coffee shop website. Again, Megan had the knowledge to link the website to others that would lead people to our site.

In fact, the site was so profitable that I've been able to pay her for her efforts. She makes a percentage of the profits from the website. This adds to her income as a realtor. She works part-time for River Valley Realtors. Megan is their top part-time seller.

On my way to the parking lot, I meandered

across the Fest Grounds. I peeked into the smallest of the three tents where musicians and dancers from all over America and Europe would perform this weekend. A sign near the entrance announced the name of this tent, Edelweiss. A quartet playing a Viennese waltz lured me in. This small tent, unlike the two bigger tents had no sides, only a net cover to keep the sun off the performers and audience.

I stopped at the bar in the back of the tent and watched two young guys doing schnapps shots with beer chasers while I waited for a wine cooler. I gave the bartender three tickets, which were used as money at all the food and drink stands.

Little booths scattered across the Fest Grounds sold tickets. Once you've paid for them, it's easy to forget what each one is worth and fest-goers tend to spend more tickets than they would cash.

I watched as he poured the wine cooler from its glass bottle into a clear plastic keg cup.

Turning, I looked for a place to sit. About a hundred folding chairs lined up like soldiers at attention in front of the stage, with only about a third of them filled. I traipsed up the center aisle and watched one lone couple waltz on the small wooden dance floor. I needed to get off my sore feet for a few minutes.

Halfway down the aisle I spotted a slender woman wearing a short navy veil with white trim, a dead giveaway. I slid into the seat next to Sister Bernadine who was dressed in her usual uniform - crisp white blouse and calf length navy blue skirt.

I had known Bernie most of my life. We had been friends, along with Megan Murphy, since first grade. On our first day of school, at recess, flirty Megan had been sitting on a swing, her arms wrapped around the swing next to her.

"Can I have that swing, Megan?" I asked.

"No. I'm saving it for William. He's going to be my boyfriend."

"He's playing ball with the other boys. Com'on, Megan, let me swing," I whined.

"No."

Little Bernie, the skinniest kid in class, walked over and grabbed the swing. "Let her have the swing or I'll smack you. You're so selfish."

A classic middle child, I tried to mediate. "Let's all be friends, okay? We can all share the swings."

I thought I was getting through to Megan about sharing when Bernie lost patience and clocked Megan in the nose. Sister Francis De Sales came running to break up the fight. By that time, the two little girls were rolling around the playground pulling each other's hair and shrieking.

I just stood on the sidelines wringing my hands and mumbling, "Oh, dear."

Our punishment had been to play together nicely for a week. We'd been best friends ever since.

Since Edwin and I separated, I've been making an effort to be more assertive. When I find myself shirking from a confrontation, I ask myself, "What would Sister Bernadine do?" I know it sounds silly but it works for me. I haven't smacked anyone yet but I had stood up to Edwin a few times.

"Bernie, are you drinking beer?"

"Oh, hello Jennifer. Well, sort of, but this isn't actually beer, it's a Radler."

"Radler? Yuck! Who drinks beer mixed with lemonade? How can you stand that nasty stuff?"

"You just don't like beer. It's more lemonade than beer anyway. My father used to give it to me when I was a girl. Besides, it's hot and this cools me off."

"To each his own." I put my feet up on the empty chair in front of me. "Who did you get into an argument with this afternoon?"

"Oh, for cripes sake, Jennifer. It was a little disagreement with someone. How in the world did you hear about it?"

"Greta the Gossip stopped by my booth." I answered; using the nickname we had called Natalie since fifth grade.

"Oh, good Lord, I suppose the whole town will hear about it. Father Werner will have me on the carpet over this. Darn it!"

"Tell me about it, maybe I can I help."

"It was nothing. A former parishioner wanted to yell at me over things that happened years ago. It wasn't important then and it certainly doesn't matter now. Don't make a big deal out of this. Look, it's almost six o'clock. Let's go watch the keg tapping." She stood up, smoothed down her skirt, and adjusted her veil.

"Nice job changing the subject, Sister." I said. We stepped out to the wide gravel road snaking through the Fest Grounds. "Okay let's go. The Civil War re-enactors will be shooting off their noisy old cannon at six o'clock sharp."

We glanced into one of the larger tents, as we strolled through the Fest Grounds and past the food stands. The scent of onion rings wafted toward us. A curly-haired little girl balanced a paper plate holding a funnel cake bathed in powered sugar as she shuffled toward a picnic table, her mother close behind.

We made a detour to the window in a tiny trailer where a bleached blonde woman wearing too much makeup sold me a paper cone filled with roasted sugared almonds. She snatched tickets from my outstretched hand and stuffed them in a drawer. She grabbed her paperback book and was back in another world before we left the booth.

Munching on nuts, we made our way to the center of the Fest Grounds to watch the keg tapping ceremony. A man wearing lederhosen, like most of the men involved in the festival as well as many of the fest-goers, rolled out a small cart holding a wooden keg that looked old and authentic. Actually, it was a metal keg purchased at the Liquor Barrel and slid into an antique-looking wooden keg cover.

Too Dead to Dance

With great ceremony and much laughter, the Fest Meister tapped the keg, and drew beer into small plastic cups for everyone.

We raised our miniature glasses, shouted *"Proust,"* and took a sip.

When the Fest Meister shouted, *"Eins, zwei, drei g'suffa,"* everyone replied with a resounding, *"Zicke, zacke, zicke, zacke, hoi, hoi, hoi!"*

It's one of the favorite German toasts at these festivities. I have no idea what it means but it's fun to shout. And even though I don't care much for beer, I caught the excitement of the festival and enthusiasm of the people who stood around the little keg. I cheered, and drank the three ounces of beer in my little cup.

A deep voice murmured in my ear. "Jennifer, we meet again."

Startled, I whipped around to look at the squat little man in green lederhosen and dribbled some beer on my t-shirt. When I saw it was Trudy's husband, I laughed and introduced him to Bernie.

"Bernie, meet Ray Neumann. His wife has that charming lace booth next to mine. Ray is the leader of one of the local bands. Ray this is Sister Bernadine."

Ray reached across and shook Bernie's hand. "Leader of the Windig Sangers, the best darn polka band in Minnesota. Nice to meet you, Sister. I've seen you at church."

Bernie's head jerked up when Ray mentioned the name of his band, and then she shook her head, stuck out her hand and said sweetly. "Are you a member of St. Theresa's Parish, Mr. Neumann?"

He pumped her hand and answered, "Please call me Ray and, yah, we've belonged to St. Theresa's since it merged with Holy Angels' Church last year. Meet some of the other members of the band."

The two Catholic churches in Hermann had merged because, although there were plenty of Catholics, there weren't enough priests. The upkeep on the two properties cost the diocese more than was taken in the collections, so the bishop had merged the two congregations. Now it didn't matter which side of town you lived on. If you wanted to go to Mass, you went to St. Theresa's, the oldest church in Maron County and the only one without air conditioning.

Ray then introduced us to Clara and Vic Schmidt. Both were members of the band. "Vic plays the clarinet and saxophone. Clara, here, is our drummer and you should hear her yodel. Sounds like she just came down from the Alps."

Clara waved her chubby hands. Pink spots appeared on her cheeks.

Ray asked, "Where are Bobby and Wes?"

"Bobby headed for the bratwurst wagon," Vic answered and pointed toward a long trailer with a sign declaring its support for the local hockey team. "He can't get enough brats and hot German potato salad. Who knows where Wes went?"

Clara crossed her arms across her bosom and huffed. "Probably to do something illegal."

Vic patted Clara on the back. "Now, Clara, be nice. Wes has had a tough life."

Clara snorted. "It's his life. He made it what it is."

I noticed the corners of Bernie's mouth turn up, just a tad, at Clara's remark.

Ray coughed and said, "He's probably in one of the tents dancing with a pretty girl. He loves to dance, that Wes."

A second later, the cannon boomed. Everybody in our small group at the keg cart jumped, and then laughed.

The Civil War re-enactors were a bunch of good old boys who loved to dress up and make noise. Like all boys, little and big, they loved speed, fire and things that go bang.

We chatted with the musicians for a while talking about past gigs and future dates. I kept looking around hoping to get a glimpse of this Wes character that had been so nasty to my friend, but he never showed up. Perhaps he saw Bernie and me with the band and kept his distance. Finally, Bernie and I left the Fest Grounds and walked to the parking lot.

5

On the way out of the Fest Grounds, we stopped for one last treat, ice cream. Tomorrow I'll eat healthy, I promised myself.

"Let's see, give me some vanilla ice cream in a paper cup. Add some sprinkles," I told the teenager behind the counter.

"I love rainbow sherbet," Bernie said. "Put mine in a sugar cone. No sprinkles."

"Sherbet in a sugar cone? Bernie, that's just not right."

"What do you know? You don't even like Radler." Laughing, we strolled through the fest grounds' exit and into the parking lot. With the music fading in the background and the evening sky on fire, the red and orange horizon ablaze, I turned to tell Bernie to look at the sunset when someone ran past us, pushing Bernie, almost knocking her down. He zigzagged between cars through the grassy parking lot. Bernie shrieked and grabbed my arm, her sherbet cone smashing into my chest.

"Are you okay?" I asked.

"Yes, did you see who it was?" Bernie, on tiptoes looked over the top of the vehicle next to her.

"No, sorry Bernie. I only got a glance at him, but he didn't look familiar. He was really tall though."

Too Dead to Dance

Bernie let out a sigh and said, "I need to get back to the church. Sorry about the mess. See you soon." Bernie scurried off to her car. I wondered why she'd left so abruptly while I brushed the pink, green, and yellow goo off my coffee, beer and now, sherbet stained shirt. I needed to buy more Tide.

I strolled toward my Civic, tired, hot, and not enthusiastic about roasting and packaging the coffee I needed for tomorrow. As I reached for the door handle, someone called my name from across the parking lot.

"Oh, no! Jennifer, can you come here?"

When I got to Bernie's car, I saw at once why she needed me. Her new little Chevy Aveo sat lopsided in the grassy parking lot. She stood shaking her head, looking at the subcompact's tires. "Well, at least they weren't slashed. Some bozo let the air out of two of my tires."

I dug my cell phone from my purse. "I'll call the police."

"Oh, good Lord, no, don't do that. Just give me a ride home and I'll call Randy to come fix it for me."

Randy Vetter and Bernie had been high school sweethearts. They had argued about everything and broke up at least once a week. When Bernie announced she would be leaving in three weeks for the convent of the Sisters of St. Ann, Randy began his campaign. He tried to convince her parents to dissuade her from leaving, but they were supporting her. He even tried to get me to come up from Illinois to "talk some sense into her," but Bernie wouldn't let anything get in the way of her vocation and her deep belief that God had called her to His service.

Randy's heartbreak didn't last long. Within a year he was married to a girl he met at community college. Lisa is an RN and works in the Emergency Room at Hermann Hospital.

Through all of this, Randy and Bernie have stayed friends. She's the Godmother to his oldest daughter and lavishes her with gifts, mostly hand made since Bernie's income is limited. Randy helps Bernie by keeping her car running.

Last fall the parishioners bought Bernie the little Aveo to celebrate her twentieth anniversary of taking her final vows. So, she hadn't needed Randy's expertise lately. I was sure he'd be glad to help her.

"Bernie, you really should report this."

"No, and that's final." She marched off toward my car. I took the hint. This subject was closed.

"Arguing with you is like pushing a boulder. I know something serious happened between you and this Wes guy. Why won't you tell me what's going on? I just want to help."

"Jennifer, I know you mean well, but I can't break a confidence. You just don't need to know about this. I'll handle it."

"Okay, but remember I'm here if you need me." "I know and I appreciate it, Jennifer."

I dropped Bernie at her apartment on Sycamore Street. I should've gone back to Primo Gusto to roast more coffee, but I was just too tired. I decided to get up early in the morning and roast the coffee I needed before leaving for the Fest Grounds. I convinced myself it would be even fresher that way.

I drove down German Street toward my new townhouse; this street meanders through Hermann. Tourists always say the first thing they notice is how tidy the town is. Like towns in Germany, the lawns are well groomed. There is no trash in the yards, there's no litter at the curbs.

When people walk around the business district, which is still an old- fashioned "downtown," German folk music plays through speakers on the lampposts.

German Street is in an area of about three square blocks that is our historical district. Built in the 1890s, these beautiful Victorian homes, Italianate mansions and lovely Queen Anne houses are a reminder of what Hermann looked like in the past. I'd love to see what the inside of that house on the corner. The yellow St. Ann with white trim looked like the crocheted doilies in Trudy's booth. A turret rose up one side and a wrap-around porch invited you to sit and rest awhile. The Hermann Historical Society put on a History Walk each fall as part of the Oktoberfest celebration. I'd have to see if this year's tour included this mansion so I could see the inside.

A few blocks further down, I came to Minnesota Street. As soon as I turned the corner, I hit the button on the remote to open the garage door. It shuddered and whined but it slowly screeched open. I pulled up the short driveway and into the garage of my townhouse.

I was still thinking about getting a bigger car, but I didn't want an SUV--too big and not fuel-efficient. I'd have to do some checking and see what would fit my needs. The door creaked and shook but finally closed. I needed to call someone to fix that.

I entered my house through the garage into the kitchen. I always came in this way. A kitchen is the easiest room to furnish. Stick in a table, chairs, toaster, and coffee pot, and it's finished. Finished but not decorated to show some of the character of the person who lived here. My kitchen was so stark the only decoration was a magnet for The Pizza Parlor in Park Rapids, Minnesota, two hundred miles north of Hermann.

It's not much different from the other rooms. When I moved in five months ago, I lined up boxes along the outside wall of my living room, thinking I'd empty them and settled in later. I hadn't opened the boxes or done anything to make it more comfortable and lived-in.

The hardwood floors were bare, not a rug in sight. When the stiff, orange sofa was delivered from a second hand shop, I just pushed it up against the inside wall. It didn't matter that it was ugly and uncomfortable. I didn't entertain and seldom even had visitors.

My only extravagances were a black leather

chair, with a matching ottoman, which sat in front of my new 42" high definition television.

Since the townhouse came with mini-blinds on the windows, I hadn't bothered to put up any curtains. I bought only the bare necessities. I kept telling myself I wanted to wait until I knew how Edwin and I would be dividing our assets before spending money on new furniture.

Okay, so there was more to it than assets and money. What I would have loved is to move into that beautiful Queen Anne mansion I had seen tonight. Of course, that was ridiculous. What would one person do in such a big house? It just seemed that it fit my style. One of the things I had brought with me from my house was an antique roll-top desk that I had retro fitted for my computer. It was clearly mine, so Edwin didn't fight me for it. And he was no fan of antiques. He thought they were just old junk.

More than furniture and this boring house, I still couldn't believe my husband had left me for another woman—a younger, beautiful woman.

Only a few months ago I thought my marriage was as good as anyone else's was, until the day Edwin dropped the bomb.

The sun had been shining through my kitchen window making the sun catcher glitter and sparkle. I picked up the spatula and flipped over a pancake in the frying pan. Edwin had liked me to cook for him, although it had been difficult with my business growing so fast. Still, I had tried to make breakfast for him most mornings.

"How do you want your eggs?" I called up the stairs to him.

"Listen, Jennie, we need to talk." Edwin came bounding down the stairs, buttoning his cuffs. He walked into the kitchen and stood by the table. Picking up a glass of orange juice, he downed it in a couple gulps.

"Don't call me Jennie," I said automatically for the thousandth time. We'd been married for twenty-four years. You'd think he'd know by now. When I was a kid, my classmates had teased me by calling me "Jennie Penny" in a singsong voice. Besides, I wanted to talk to him about him about an offer I had received for my business but he wouldn't let me talk.

"Jennifer, don't interrupt me. I have something important to say. I know this is going to be difficult for you, but now that Beth is married and Nick has moved to Chicago, I need my freedom."

I shook my head and wiped my hands on a dishcloth. "What are you talking about? Do you want to make Nick's room into a den?"

"No, I don't want to move furniture. Jennifer, I want a divorce. It's time for me to have a life of my own. I need to find out who I am."

I thought I was going to throw up. My feelings poured out of my mouth. "What? I worked every day of this marriage, too. After I put you through college, I raised the kids while you belonged to every club in town and spent your evenings at meetings. I'm the one who went to PTA, piano recitals, and scout meetings. And now you want to leave?" I had never talked to Edwin like this in my life. "You want find out who you are? You're a louse, that's who you are."

Then it hit me. How stupid I had been. "Who is she?"

"Now, Jennie, don't be that way."

"Don't you 'Now, Jennie' me, you creep. I know you. This didn't just come to you in a dream. Besides, you could never take care of yourself. Who would make your breakfast?"

"Okay. Enough. I'm moving out. My lawyer will contact your lawyer. I'm using Dyson & Dyson. You should call Erickson, Lowe, and Jones. They'd be a good firm for you."

He picked up an overnight bag, which I hadn't notice him bringing down the stairs and walked out the front door.

I followed him, still not believing what was happening. "Don't you tell me who my lawyer should be. In fact, don't you ever tell me anything again. From now on, I'll be doing as I damn please, just like you've always done."

"Fine. My lawyer is setting up a little allowance for you. Don't run up a lot of charges. Also, you had better start looking for a real job. I don't plan to get stuck with the bills from your coffee hobby after I'm gone. And you'd better start looking for a place to live. I'm putting the house on the market today." Edwin tossed his bag into his silver Mazda Miata. That flashy new car should've been a tip-off. I sure could be dense at times.

I had seldom stood up to Edwin, but he'd never left me before, either. There was more to it than that. Why hadn't I cried, I thought? I had been pissed but not sad or heartbroken.

I felt comfortable here in my hometown, while Edwin believed his company had banished to the boondocks. That must be where I got the gumption to stand up to him. And his feelings must be the reason he felt the need to cheat on me. As I sat there trying to take it all in, a sense of relief had washed over me. Now sadness clutched my heart as I remembered our first years together when we were young and in love.

I knew I needed to get over the feelings of abandonment and get on with my life. Okay, so Edwin never qualified for the perfect husband award. An overbearing control freak, he made all the decisions for the family. I seldom question his decisions. He had often let me know my opinion didn't matter to him.

"I earn the money to support this family, Jennie. You just stay home with the kids. You don't have any idea of what happens in the real world."

He was a good father. The kids and I never went without anything, but his word was law and he'd make a proclamation then slap his hand on the table to stress the point.

I sat down, put my feet up, and thought about my marriage. I hadn't thought of it as being much different from anyone else's marriage. Edwin acted much like my father, except Edwin didn't go to work drunk and get fired. When the shock of his leaving wore off, I took a good look at my life and decided life was much easier without him. I just couldn't help feeling as if somehow I had failed. And sometimes I got so lonely.

Shaking off these contradictory feelings, I made myself a promise to go shopping soon. After Edwin and I met with the divorce mediator next week, I'd decorate this place so it would be homier. Or maybe I wouldn't renew my lease. I could go out and find a house to fit my personality. Not this sterile little box.

This place was nice, well maintained, and had absolutely no character. The house Edwin and I had purchased here in Hermann was new but inside it had the feel of a farmhouse. It had big rooms, lots of wood and windows. I had decorated all the rooms in a traditional style and, except for the formal living room, which we never used, it felt homey and comfortable. I mostly missed my bathroom. The master bedroom had an amazing bathroom. Two sinks, a walk -in shower surrounded in glass with four showerheads and a deep two-person Jacuzzi tub. I could have lived in there.

Feeling lonely, I made a quick call to my friend, Megan. Her phone rang and finally went to voice mail. I hung up. She was probably talking to her current boyfriend. I sent a text message to her cell phone for her to call me when she got a chance.

After showering off the fest dust, I donned my Sponge Bob sleep shirt and curled up with my current book, a Joanne Fluke mystery.

Trying to forget Bernie's problems and feeling sorry for myself, I ate a chocolate chip cookie I had bought at the Fest. I read the same page twice without comprehending anything. I couldn't stop worrying about

Bernie. Sure, she was tough; she stood up for people all the time. Why had she practically run off tonight? It was so unlike her. There was more going on than she was willing to tell me. I worried for her safety.

I vowed to call her tomorrow and grill her about this Wes guy. I'd also ask Trudy if she could tell me anything she knew about him. At least I could find out his last name. Maybe I'd have a little talk with him, too.

I clicked off the television, which I wasn't watching anyway and was about to go to bed when the phone rang. Thinking it must be Megan; I picked up the receiver and said, "Hi, I'm sure glad you called."

"Well, I'm glad, you're glad," answered a woman's voice that wasn't Megan.

"Who is this?" I asked.

Laughing the lady answered, "Its Laura from the Biergarten Restaurant in Mankato."

"I'm so sorry, Laura. I thought you were my neighbor. I've been waiting for her to return my call."

"That's okay, Jennifer. I'm sorry to call so late, but I have a favor to ask of you."

"What can I do for you?"

"I have a favor to ask of you. I saw this fantastic German beer stein in Hermann a couple weeks ago. And like an idiot, I didn't buy it. I've been thinking about it ever since and I just have to have it! I know I saw it in Hermann but I can't remember where. Can you help me?"

"I'm sure I can, Laura," I said, thinking about how much extra work this might entail. "What does it look like?"

"It's the coolest stein I've ever seen! It's a Coca-Cola stein with a scene from an old -fashioned ice cream soda fountain on it. It looks like an old German beer stein. If I email you a picture could you look for it for me?"

"Well, I guess I can try," I said without much enthusiasm."

"Listen, Jennifer, I know this is an imposition on

you. If you can do this for my I'd love to have you and a friend come down here for a Surf and Turf dinner for two."

That perked me up. I love lobster. "Surf and turf doesn't sound very German to me. When did you put that on your menu?"

"A few months ago. We're the best restaurant in Worthington and people like to come here for special occasions. So, we added a few special items to the menu. Do you like steak and lobster?"

"You betcha. What kind of turf?"

"Only the best Filet Mignon. Does that motivate you?

"Absolutely! I'd be glad to give it a try, Laura." Now that's the kind of motivation I liked. "Send me the picture and description and I'll see what I can do. Also, can you list the places you went to on the day you saw it? That will give me some place to start looking."

"I'll email you the details right away. I have to think about where I was. Seems to me I was all over town."

"Well, do your best, Laura, and I'll see what I can find."

"Thanks, Jennifer, I really appreciate this."

Laura's email came through in just a few minutes. I printed it out along with the picture she had attached. Laura was one of my best customers. Her German restaurant was upscale and people drove from all over southern Minnesota to dine there I looked at the picture of the stein. It was lovely. I could understand why she wanted to add it to her collection. She had over a hundred mugs and steins displayed in her restaurant.

The list she sent me of the places she went to the day she saw the stein wasn't too long. I went online to the Hermann Chamber of Commerce site to find the addresses of the places Laura said she had visited the day she saw the stein. I looked at the list Laura had sent me. Zeller's Antiques topped the list. There was a second-hand shop downtown, Oma's Attic. The list also included Bavarian Haus, Glessener's German Store, and Messer's Coins to Cups. List in hand; I was ready to begin my search.

Somehow, I'd find time tomorrow to start looking for this interesting stein. Maybe I could get Bernie to come with me. I might be able to find out what was bothering her. Dragging myself out of my easy chair, I shuffled off to bed. Megan hadn't called back and I wasn't going to wait up for her to get home. Lord only knew when that might be. My thoughts turned to a steak and lobster dinner and I fell into a deep sleep.

Too Dead to Dance

6

Friday

Jennifer!" Jacobs' deep voice brought me back to the fest grounds and the shocking event of finding a dead body this morning.

"Was Sister Bernadine's car here when you got back this morning?"

I had to admit it wasn't. "Randy is our mechanic and friend. Sister Bernadine must have called him to come out and air up her tires."

Jacobs took down Randy's name and phone number in his little notebook.

He looked down the gravel drive running through the fairgrounds and watched a blue van approach. It pulled up behind Jacobs' car.

A curvaceous young woman in tight jeans and a blue shirt with the State of Minnesota emblem over the pocket jumped out of the van and approached Detective Decker. Over her long fingers, she donned a pair of latex gloves. Grabbing her long blonde hair, she pulled it back and wrapped a scrunchie around her ponytail. She gave Detective Decker a sexy smile. "Hi, Jer, Where do you want us?"

Decker waved a hand toward the building then followed her through the door. I heard him say, "It's

Too Dead to Dance

Jerry, not Jer."

The coroner came out, and arrogantly strode towards his car. All he had to do was pronounce the man dead. I could've done that an hour ago.

I waved to Bernie when I saw her crossing the road near the grandstand, just down from the Home Arts building.

Before I could say anything, Detective Decker walked out of the Home Arts building and made a beeline toward us. "Sister Bernadine?"

"Yes," she said a puzzled look on her face. "What's going on?"

"I'm Detective Decker. I need to ask you a few questions. Would you mind coming down to the Sheriff's Office with me?"

"I guess it would be alright." Looking at me she asked, "Has something happened?"

Decker gently touched her shoulder and guiding her toward the squad car, he said, "I'll explain everything at the station. We need to go now." With that, Detective Decker swooped her off to the Sheriff's Office for questioning.

Jacobs left me sitting outside the Home Arts Building again while he questioned a bunch of other people. I shamelessly eavesdropped as Jacobs questioned Trudy's husband Ray.

"Don't you think it's a pretty big coincidence that Wes, a member of your band, was killed right next to your wife's booth?"

Ray replied, "I don't know what Wes was doing in there. Trudy had nothing to do with this. She was with me."

"When was she with you, Ray?" Jacobs asked.

"All night. She came to the big tent about nine o'clock to watch me play and we went home together from there. We didn't even stop to eat with the rest of the band. Trudy was tired. It was a long day for her."

"Where does the band usually go to eat, Ray"

"The only place that's open at that time of night.

Dottie's Diner."

"And all the other band members went there last night?"

"I don't know. We went home. Trudy was tired."

"What about you, Ray? Were you tired, too? Or did you go out for a little drive after your wife went to sleep?"

"No! I never left the house until I came here this morning to drop her off. I don't even start playing until eleven."

When he finished with Ray, he turned to a sandy-haired lanky young guy.

"Are you Bobby Reinhardt?" Detective Jacobs asked. Since they were a little closer to me, I leaned forward, tipped my head down. With My hand on my forehead and elbow on my knee, I could hear what was being said, and hoped I looked deep in thought instead of surreptitiously listening.

Jacobs asked. "So, how well did you know Wes?"

"Not very well."

"Come on, Bobby. This is Hermann, everybody knows everyone else here."

"Yeah, well, I knew him. I knew he was a jerk, but I didn't hang with him or anything."

Jacobs made a note in his little notebook. "Heard you two banged heads a couple times."

"Yeah. He was dancing with my sister the other night and it pissed me off. She should know better."

"What should she know?"

"That Wes is—was—an ex-con. I don't know why Bridget always goes after those types of guys."

"What type is that, Bobby?"

"Bridget calls them bad boys. I call them jerks." Bobby's lip curled on one side.

"Okay. I heard you also had some words with him about your girlfriend."

"My girlfriend doesn't like him. She acts like she's scared of him, so I told him to stay away from her."

"Did she tell you why she's afraid of him?"

"No. And I asked. She just said . . ." Bobby's

voice trailed off when he shifted his position and Jacobs moved right in front of him. I couldn't hear anything they said.

When Jacobs finally got back to me, I repeated what I had seen in the parking lot, again leaving out what Bernie had told me about the argument with Wes. After all, I hadn't witnessed it. "I can't believe you're considering Sister Bernadine as a suspect in this. She's a nun, for Pete's sake."

"Jennifer, I know you want to believe she's above reproach. I know you think bad things can't happen in a small town. In the years I've been a cop, I've seen a lot of ugly things. People are people, small town or large; there are people capable of the most heinous things."

"I believe that, Lieutenant Jacobs. Remember, I'm the one who found the body, but I've known Sister Bernadine most of my life. She's outspoken and sometimes tactless, but she'd never hurt another human being. She just couldn't do that."

"That may be true. Detective Decker will get her alibi and check her off the list."

When I was finally ready to leave, the paramedics wheeled a gurney out of the building. Glancing at the shiny black body bag, I shivered, spilling some water down the front of my perky pink top.

"Lieutenant Jacobs, is there some way I could get my coffee from the building? I hate to leave it there overnight."

"I'll get it for you, Jennifer. Just pull your car up here."

I backed away from Jacobs and made my way to my Civic. I was glad Detective Decker had left with Bernie before he could see my moist tush.

When I pulled my car up to the Home Arts building, Jacobs was busy talking to a group of vendors. When he saw me, he said. "Jennifer, go in and get the box of coffee but don't touch anything else. Okay?"

Walking into the building, I felt the hair on my

arms rise. Then the stench hit me. I covered my nose and mouth and hurried over to my table. I held my breath and hoisted the box of coffee. Then I spotted the white bakery bag I'd flung across the booth crunched up in the corner. I wondered who could've been so callous to eat a stolen donut in front of a blood soaked corpse. My money was on the smart-mouthed EMT.

When I came out of the building Jacobs was talking to Clara and Vic also members of Trudy's husband's band.

Clara said, "We stopped for a bite to eat at Dottie's Diner after we left the Fest Grounds. It must have been about midnight. No one else from our band showed up so we sat with a band from Texas."

"Texas?" Jacobs asked. "Is that someplace in Germany?"

Vic and Clara laughed and Vic said, "People always ask that. Actually, there is a large community of people of German decent in and around Fredericksburg, Texas. It's actually larger than the German population here in southwest Minnesota."

"Did you see leave with anyone after you finished playing for the night?"

"No," Clara said. "He jumped down off the bandstand carrying his trumpet and walked into the crowd and that's the last I saw of him. He didn't even stick around to help pack up the instruments. As usual. I think he might have gone to the other tent. He liked to dance and that tent stays open until midnight."

I excused myself for interrupting and told Jacobs I was leaving I thanked him for letting me get my coffee. He assured me the building could open tomorrow as usual. I didn't want to go into that building again but I had signed a contract to keep my booth open until six o'clock Sunday evening. The coffee would still be fresh tomorrow and if anyone showed up, maybe I could sell most of it. Fifty pounds of coffee I wouldn't be selling today sat in the back seat of my car. I guess I was lucky

Too Dead to Dance

the deputies hadn't confiscated it.

7

I called Bernie's apartment from my cell phone and left a message for her to call me as soon as Detective Decker finished grilling her. Since I couldn't open my booth today, I decided to start looking for Laura's beer stein.

Glancing at the list, I decided that I'd start at the antique store. I pulled into a diagonal parking space in front of the Built for Speed bicycle shop in downtown Herman, next door to Zeller's Antiques. I glanced into the bike shop and saw Bernie standing at the counter talking to a young guy.

I waited until she walked out then greeted her. "I see that they didn't lock you up. Are you okay?"

"I'm fine, Jennifer."

"What did the police say to you? Are you sure you're okay?"

"Jennifer, I'm fine. I don't want to talk about it. Okay?"

"Okay, fine," I decided I'd better change the subject, for now. "Do you still have that old bike?" Bernie was quite a sight peddling around Hermann in a forty-year-old Schwinn bicycle with a wire basket, which held her canvas bag. "I thought you got rid of it when the parishioners bought you the new car?"

"No, I got rid of the old car. I still love to ride my

bike. It's the only bike I ever owned. I got it for my fourteenth birthday. I did need to order some new gloves," she said holding up a plastic bag with "Built for Speed" and a bicycle printed on it.

"Want to come with me? I'm looking for a beer stein for a customer and want to check out Zellers." I thought I might be able to get her relaxed enough to tell me what happened to her at the sheriff's department.

"Sure, why not." She shrugged and turned with me to check out the antique store.

I was pleasantly surprised when we walked into Zeller's Antiques. I expected a dimly lit, dusty room filled with heavy old furniture. Instead, it looked more like a modern furniture store.

The first thing I saw was a dining room set. A large table with eight matching chairs was set with flowery Bavarian china. Behind the table, a heavy sideboard with a pair of matching lamps stood watch over the table.

As we walked through the store, I looked at the other room settings. The pieces didn't always match but they complemented each other. It gave the store a comfortable feel; a place where you wanted to spend some time just looking around. "Isn't this a lovely store?" I asked Bernie.

"It's a very nice store," she answered. "Too bad the proprietor isn't as nice."

"What do you mean?" I asked while looking at a beautiful sideboard with a matching mirror.

Just then, a slender young man wearing jeans, a grey blazer with patches on the elbows and a dark blue tie made his way through the furniture. Pushing his glasses up on his nose he said, "Hello, I'm Thomas Zeller. May I help you find something?"

"Your store is beautiful. I've already seen several items I'd like to have in my home." If I had a home, I thought. "What I'm looking for is a beer stein."

"We have several steins, let me show them to you," he said with a sweep of his arm toward a tall

Diane Morlan

hutch with glass doors. Wine glasses filled three shelves. The bottom shelf held several china knick-knacks and three squat, colorful beer steins with pewter lids. None of them had the Coca-Cola logo.

"Here's a picture of the stein I'm looking for," I said handing him the picture Laura had sent me.

When he looked at the picture, his eyebrows crawled up his face toward his hairline and his head jerked back as if he was trying to get away from the paper in his hand. "This is not an antique! I would never carry something like this."

I pulled the paper from his hand and put it back in my purse. "You don't carry any collectables?"

"Of course not. This is an antique store," he replied. "Do you know where I might find this stein?" I thought he might have some connections that could be useful to me.

"Try a flea market." He said and stuck his nose up in the air.

"Okay well, thank you."

I looked at Bernie who just shrugged and turned toward the front door. I began to follow her when my eyes again went to the sideboard. It was a fat, heavy buffet embellished with curly ques. Three slender drawers lined the top front of the piece and were perfect for silverware. The three deep drawers that sat under them could hold table linens. Two large doors on each side would hold china and a myriad of items.

"Just a minute, Bernie," I said and walked over to the buffet and when I ran my hand over the dark wooden top I noticed the chocolate marble inlays. This piece would look wonderful in a Victorian dining room. I patted the top as if to say, "I'll be back for you," and made my way through the other pieces to the door.

Outside Bernie said, "I told you he wasn't very nice. If he didn't have a God-given talent for procuring the best items and the ability to show them at their finest, he'd have gone out of business years ago. Sorry, Jennifer, snobs annoy me."

Too Dead to Dance

"That's okay, I have to get going. Would you like a ride home?" I was thinking that getting her in my car would be a good time to talk to her. That way she couldn't get away from me.

She pointed toward her bike, "Nope, have my own transportation."

"I'll call you later. I need to talk to you."

"I'll call you, Jennifer. I have a couple stops to make."

Back in my car, I crossed Zeller's Antiques off my list. Zeller was a pompous ass, but he sure had some beautiful furniture in his shop. I wanted that sideboard. I really wanted that sideboard. All I needed was the right home for it.

I stopped at Stanley's market and picked up some bread, milk and a few other items, then decided to go home I called Bernie's apartment but there was no answer, no voice mail either. She should have been home by now. My phone rang almost as soon as I snapped it shut. "Bernie, where are you?"

"It's not Bernie, it's me, Megan. What the hell have you gotten yourself into now?"

"Oh, Lord, Megan I'm so glad it's you," I said, relieved that she'd finally returned my phone call. "Why didn't you call me back last night?"

"It was late when I got home. Your lights were off and I didn't want to wake you. What's up?"

I told her about the events of the day, then added, "Not only did I find a dead body but I found a live one I don't know what to do with."

"You met a man? I'll be right over. Don't go anywhere."

Two minutes later, she bounded through my front door, slamming it behind her. Carrying two wine coolers, she handed one to me and plopped down on my sofa. "Okay, Sweetie, tell me all the goodies. Who's the guy? Do I know him?"

"His name is Jerry Decker. He's a cop, a detective, I think."

"Oh, yeah. I heard about him. One of the realtor's in my office, Sherri, I think, found him a house to rent. He's only been here a few months. Word is he's hot. Is he?"

I described my reaction to Jerry Decker and his winking at me as if we shared a secret. "I'm so not ready for this, Megan. Help me."

"Gee, Jennifer, I hate to tell you this but there's no help for a physical attraction like yours. Either it wears off after a short physical relationship or it moves into something more important. It depends on the character and intentions of the participants."

"Stop with the psychological analysis and tell me what to do."

"Jump in bed with him, Sweetie. It's the only way to get him out of your system."

"Megan, I certainly have no intention of getting into bed with anyone." I could feel my spine stretch out as I sat up straighter. "Besides, he's at least five years younger than I am. And he makes me stutter." I wailed.

Megan had the nerve to sit there and snicker. "Who cares about age these days? Don't you know it's cool to date younger men? They call them cougars." She laughed and lightly punched me in the arm

"Who's called cougars?"

"Women who date younger men are called cougars. It's fashionable to date young guys."

"Right. I live to be fashionable."

"Face it, Sweetie. You've got it bad already. The bug has bitten you."

I could've slapped her. Well, no I couldn't. Not really. She's my best friend, even though she pulls no punches with me. After so many years of Edwin's browbeating, I knew I didn't want to get involved with anyone for any reason, at least, not right now.

"Oh, good Lord," I groaned. "I'm not even divorced yet."

"You know, Edwin isn't divorced from you either and he has no problem getting involved with someone else."

"Edwin is scum," I retorted.

"True. So, what about the dead dude? What's going on with that?"

"Oh, Megan, it was awful seeing that bloody body. We need to find the fool who killed this Wes guy to get Bernie off the hook."

"Bernie? You mean both of you are involved in this mess? I don't know how you get mixed-up in these things, Jennifer. Why do you even have a coffee booth at Polka Daze? You said you got an offer to sell Primo Gusto?"

"Oh, I did, but I just don't know what to do. One day I feel that I can't refuse the offer that company in Seattle made me, and then I don't know how I can part with it. In any case, my lawyer says to wait until the divorce is final to make a decision so Edwin can't get any of the profits."

"Didn't he sign off on the incorporation so he couldn't be held liable for your debts?" Megan asked

"Yes and he hasn't been any part of my business. But, if I sell before the divorce is final, he may be able to get some of the money I receive from the sale."

"Well, then you'd better wait to sell. You built the business, with him fighting you every step along the way. He doesn't deserve to get any of the profits."

"I'm not even sure I want to sell. Primo Gusto is like my child. It's complicated."

"Isn't everything? Remember you were interested in selling before Edwin left you. Maybe you just need it now while you heal. Promise me you won't make a decision until you work out your feelings about the divorce and where you want to go from here."

I was getting some pressure from the company in Seattle that made the offer but I put them off until after the divorce, so I have some time to decide what to do,"

"That's good. Okay, what do we have to do to help Bernie?"

I watched as Megan downed the last of her

cooler. I had only taken a few sips of mine.

"When Bernie and I were walking toward our cars after the keg tapping, this guy ran into us. He almost knocked Bernie down. I think it was Wes."

"Why do you think it was Wes?" Megan asked. "Because he was tall and he hid his face and who else would try to knock down a nun? When Bernie got to her car, she found both tires on the driver's side were flat. They weren't cut, they we just flat. I think Wes let the air out of them."

"That's no help. If this Wes dude flattened her tires, it gives her more reason to knock him off. We need to find out what the argument was all about."

"Okay, so where were you last night? Is Don in town?" I asked. Don Dahlberg was Megan's current love interest. An airline pilot, he was only in Hermann a few days a week, which is probably why the relationship had lasted for over three months.

Megan rolled her eyes at me. "It was the first night of Polka Daze. Where else would I be but in the big tent until it closed."

"Oh, good Lord, you must have seen Wes! He was in the Windig Sangers Band."

"I probably did. Actually, I wasn't paying too much attention to the people on the stage. I was busy with the guy sitting next to me."

"Don? How did you drag him to Polka Daze? He hates that music."

"Don's in Reno. I went alone but hooked up with a guy—a young, good-looking guy. Are you going to drink this?" she asked reaching for my wine cooler.

Handing her my bottle I asked, "How can you cheat on Don? I thought it was the real thing this time."

"Maybe it is, I don't know. All I do know is that I was lonely and Al was there and he was so cute—and young."

"How young?" I asked.

"I don't know. I didn't check his ID. He was flirty and cute and it was fun. Guess you can call me a cougar, too."

"I can't believe you cheated on Don? How could you?"

"Hey! Don't go getting on my case. I'm not Edwin or Marty. I'm not married and I not in an exclusive relationship, I can do as I please!"

It was time for me to shut up. She might be right. Maybe I was projecting Edwin on her, but I hate cheating, it's so low.

Changing the subject, I asked her what else she knew about Detective Decker.

"Not much. He's somewhat of a mystery. He moved here a couple months ago to take the detective job when Harvey Marshall retired. I got my hair done last week and one of the girls at Hair Haus told her customer that he came from Chicago. That seems to be about all anyone knows. She said he lives alone and apparently, he doesn't party. He sounds boring, if you ask me."

I guess I had asked her. Personally, I didn't think that someone was boring just because he didn't hang out in bars. Of course, I didn't say that to Megan. "Okay, so we need to figure out how to help Bernie."

"Jennifer, I have no idea how to catch a killer. You're the one who watches all those crime shows on TV."

"We need to find out what the argument between Bernie and Wes was all about. Do you think she'd tell you? She clammed up on me last night when I asked. Of course that was before he got killed."

"I can try. I'll go over to her place tomorrow and see if I can get her to talk," she said.

"I'll try to find out about Wes. I can start with Trudy, the Lady with the booth next to mine. Her husband leads the band and probably hired Wes. If she can't help me maybe, she can tell me who can. We can compare notes later tomorrow and figure out where to go from there."

Megan downed the last of my wine cooler and

grabbed the empty bottles. "I'm outta here," she said moving toward the front door. "Off to the Fest Grounds for more fun and games."

"Have fun," I called to her. "Behave yourself."
"Make up your mind, Jennifer. I can't do both." She waved and shut the door.

Too Dead to Dance

8

I went to the kitchen for a cup of coffee. When I saw the magnet on the fridge advertising a pizza place in Park Rapids, MN, I thought about my daughter, Beth. She'd gone to Hermann High School for her senior year where she met Ken Trager. They got married right after graduation. Beth and Ken were living "up North" as Minnesotans say when referring to any place north of the Twin Cities.

They ran a resort near Park Rapids and the owner told them he'd give them first chance to buy if he decided to sell. They spent the summer renting, cleaning, and maintaining the cabins and grounds. During the winter months, they made repairs, shoveled snow, and rented cabins to hunters.

Maybe Beth knew Wes. He was older than she was but girls always knew the older guys. Or not. Given what Megan had said about cougars, maybe that wasn't true anymore.

Ken answered the phone and when Beth got on the line I explained what had happened to Bernie, I asked her about Wes. "I didn't know him, Mom. Oh, I knew about him. He's older and was already out of school when we moved here. He hung around with a bunch of other dropouts who were always getting into trouble. My friends and I stayed away from that bunch

Too Dead to Dance

of losers. I do remember the bank robbery, though. Maybe Nick knows more about him."

Nick is my son. He's two years older than Beth and was in college at Northern Illinois University when we moved here. He decided to stay in Illinois, but spent summers with us until he graduated. Now he works as an accountant. Unlike his father, he's working toward an MBA. He has a great job as a comptroller at a riverboat casino in northern Indiana, a few miles from the Illinois border.

"I doubt if Nick knows him. He didn't spend much time here, but I'll give him a call."

"Are you okay, Mom? It must have been gross to find a dead body. Yuck."

"Well, it sure wasn't pleasant. The worst part is that the police are looking at Sister Bernadine as a suspect." "Oh, Mom, that's just crazy. She couldn't hurt a flea. She was such a big help to me when I was getting ready for my wedding."

"She was?" I asked. "I don't seem to remember her being so helpful. She wasn't even around much. Didn't she have that summer Bible day camp for teens about that time?"

"Yes, she did. But I needed her wisdom, not her hands."

"Beth, what are you talking about?"

"Well, you know. It was getting close to the wedding, the invitations were out, the flowers were ordered, and everyone was so busy when I suddenly thought, 'What the hell and I doing?' I had all these fears and was ready to run away. So, I went to see Sister Bernie and she told me to look at what I wanted from life. She said not to be influenced by what others wanted for me but to think about what I wanted from my life."

"Did that help? I never knew..."

"Yes, it did. We prayed together then she let me know that what I was feeling was normal and not to worry. She assured me that marrying Ken was a good thing and that I wouldn't regret it. She was right. I've never been happier."

"Wow! I never knew you had the last minute jitters. You acted so unruffled."

"I was unruffled after I talked to Sister Bernie."

"Why didn't you come to me, Beth?" I asked.

"Oh, Mom. You were practically a basket case with all the details to attend to. I didn't want to get you all freaked out, too."

"I wouldn't have been 'freaked out', as you put it. I could have told you—"

"You could have told me a lot of things, but I didn't want to put more pressure on you. You were so busy and I didn't want to disappoint you. It all worked out fine."

"Oh alright, I see your point," I said, not really seeing the point. I was her mother, after all. "I don't understand what made you decide to talk to Bernie? She obviously didn't have any personal experience in that area."

"Oh, yes she did. She left her family and friends and went into the convent while practically everyone in her life was trying to change her mind. I knew she'd understand. And even though I love Megan, I think I was afraid to confide in her because she might have told me to bail. I wanted to marry Ken. I think I just needed someone to tell me I was doing the right thing."

"I never knew," I stammered.

"You weren't supposed to, Mom. You had enough to worry about."

"How is everything going way up there in the north woods?" I asked, changing the subject.

"Great. We had an ultrasound yesterday and you can actually see the baby! I'll scan it and email it to you. It's awesome. You know, you need to get a Facebook page so you can see all the pictures of Ken and me and the resort."

"I know, Honey but it's so much work. And I'm so busy."

Too Dead to Dance

"Mom. It'll only take ten minutes. And you'll be glad you did once you get it done. Have Megan get you signed up if you don't know what to do. She's a whiz with computers and online stuff."

I bristled. "I don't need Megan to help me. I'm sure I can follow the instructions and get signed up. After all, every seventh grader is on Facebook."

"Okay. I'll look for your friend request." I'm sure I heard her giggle.

"Mom, there's something else I want to talk to you about, but I'm not sure I should."

"Oh, Beth, you know you can tell me anything," I said, surprised again that she was reluctant to share with me. She'd never had a problem telling me her secrets, or had she? I only knew what she told me, not what she chose not to share.

"Daddy came up here last weekend."

"That's terrific. I'm sure you had a good time. I don't want you to take sides, Beth. Our problems are between us. We don't want you and Nick to feel that you have to choose between us. We both love you."

"I know that, Mom. The problem is that he brought his girlfriend with him. I didn't know what to do."

"You mean Marty? I know about her. I hope you were nice to her." I knew about the new girlfriend. She was a waitress at one of the restaurants that bought coffee from me.

"It wasn't Marty that I was upset with. For cripes sake, she's almost as young as me!"

"Your father is going through a mid-life crisis. I think he feels that he's getting old. The new flashy car and the young flashy girlfriend make him feel young again."

"How can you be so nice about it? I think it's horrible and I wanted to yell at him."

"Well, don't yell at him, I already did that. It didn't do any good. Just give him some time. You two have always been so close. Don't lose that feeling."

"Mom, that closeness ended a long time ago. Actually, Daddy's been different since we moved to Hermann. I just don't know what's up with him."

"I don't know either, Sweetie. But he's your father so be nice to him."

"I will and I was but it was such an uncomfortable situation. I gave them a cottage to use while they were here. I couldn't bear to have them sleep together in my house. Gross! Now I know why you wouldn't let Ken sleep over before we got married."

"I'm sorry that he put you in such an awkward situation, Beth."

"It was more than awkward, Mom. The second night they were here, Ken and I went for a walk before we went to bed. When we went past their cottage, we heard Daddy yelling at her. Marty was yelling back and I could tell she was crying, too. It sounded like they were arguing about money. I could hardly look at them at breakfast the next morning."

"I'm sure you were your usual polite self, dear."
"Polite, yes but not friendly. I was relieved when they left. I love him and was really looking forward to his visit but I wish he had come alone."

"Beth, have you thought that maybe he was looking for your approval?"

"My approval? When did I become the parent?"
"These things are very complicated. Our emotions get all mixed up with our expectations. Just hang in there. It will all sort itself out. Try to be patient with him."

"I don't know what to do when he wants to come up again."

"I'm sure you and Ken will figure it out, Beth."
"Mom, do you think you and Daddy will get back together?"

"No, Honey, it's over for us. Too much water under the bridge and all that, you know?"

"Yeah, I know. Part of me would like things to go back how they were. I think you're happier now that he's out of your life. Are you seeing anyone? I mean, it's none of my business, but—"

"No, I'm not dating, yet. I suppose I probably will eventually. I'm just not ready to get involved with anyone yet. I'm enjoying the freedom to do as I please."

"Well, when you start dating, find a guy like Ken. Then you can still do as you please. He's the best."

After we hung up, I found the Facebook Home page and set up my account. Beth was right; it only took a few minutes. I spent the next hour looking for people I knew and sending out friends requests.

I finally remembered to call Nick. When I punched his number into my cell, it went right to voice mail. Nick must have turned it off. I left a brief message asking him to call me when he got a chance. And since I was still sitting at the computer desk, I sent him an email briefly describing the events of the day and asking him if he'd ever run into Wes during his summers in Hermann.

I set the phone down and jumped as it immediately rang. Caller I.D. showed it was Bernie, at last. "Are you okay?" I asked without even saying "Hello."

"I'm fine, Jennifer."

"I thought you'd call back sooner. I was worried that the police had picked you up again."

"I believe once a day is enough, Jennifer. I'm just tired and cranky. Right now, I'm on my way over to the rectory. Father Werner wants to meet for 'a little talk.' I can only imagine how unpleasant that'll be."

"Can't you put him off until tomorrow? You must be bushed."

Father Werner, old, stubborn, and cantankerous, ruled his dwindling realm with a heavy hand. Most of the people involved in the parish were volunteers. Only Sister Bernadine and three administrative assistants were on the payroll.

"No, you know how he is. I'd just as soon get it over with, or I'll worry about it all night. After he bawls me out, I can go home and get some sleep. I'll talk to you tomorrow."

I couldn't think of anything to say, so I thanked her for calling and let her go. I dug receipts from expenses and sales out of my purse. As usual, I had been stuffing them in my purse for the past week. I needed to enter them into my ledger so my accountant didn't give me another lecture.

I knew I needed to send out "past due" notices to several restaurants whose payments were overdue but it was a task I didn't relish. A few businesses were always late in paying me.

The restaurant business could be dicey. One day they are the "in" place to go until next week when diners move on to another place. Also, when the economy fluctuates dining out is the first thing people cut in order to save money. I'm good about arranging with these businesses and had kept my customers while they went through tough times.

I heated up some left over sweet and sour pork in the microwave and half-heartedly ate some supper. My drink of choice is hot coffee with a dollop of cream. Although in theory I'm generally against caffeine-free anything, I chose to go the caffeine-free coffee route this late in the evening or I'd never get to sleep. I kept thinking about Bernie being so stubborn. Why was she being so secretive about the fight with Wes?

And what about this Detective Decker? Why was I so attracted to him? I went back to the computer and Googled his name.

I found several articles in the Chicago Tribune about him. Sergeant Decker received numerous awards for bravery from the Chicago Police Department. He'd been a volunteer at the Chicago Boys Club and several other local youth programs.

It appeared that he was quite involved in his job and his community. Why would he leave there to move to Hermann?

Further down I noticed a story about a trial that took place about a year ago. One of the witnesses was

Too Dead to Dance

Detective Jerome Decker. What had happened to Sergeant Decker, I wondered. Checking Wikipedia, I found that in Chicago a Detective isn't a ranking officer. It appeared that Detective Decker had been demoted. Curious, very curious.

I was so tired my eyes were starting to cross. I'd have to search for more information about Detective Decker another time. I turned off the computer and went to my bedroom. I donned my Betty Boop pajamas and thought about what I would be wearing if Jerry Decker were here.

"Stop!" I told myself, I didn't need those images in my head keeping me awake.

9

Saturday

Reaching into the trunk of my Civic, I pulled out the folding crate on wheels I had picked up at Office Max on my way to the Fest Grounds. I swore I'd never use one of these wire "granny" carts my mother had embarrassed me by pushing all over town. I was grateful when I found this file box cart. I couldn't deal with lugging heavy boxes across the Fest Grounds one more time. I looked down at my shoes and although the bleach had taken out the bloodstain, I could still see it. I thought I might have to go shopping soon and get another new pair of sneakers.

To my surprise, without the struggle of carrying forty pounds of coffee bags, I enjoyed the hike across the Fest Grounds. Potted flowers were everywhere. Bright red azaleas, purple hydrangeas, and salmon-colored impatiens danced in flowerpots lining the walkway and clustered at the entrances to tents and buildings.

Workers were setting up their food stands and the smell of flowers mixed with the odor of hot grease. I turned the corner and had the Home Arts Building in sight when I heard someone call my name.

"Jennifer, wait up! I want to ask you something."

I knew that voice. Damn. "Hello, Natalie." I said, catching myself from calling her Greta. "I'm in a bit of a hurry. I seem to be late."

She skipped into step next to me. Today she wore an azure tank top neatly tucked into her spotless, crisp white Capri pants, and again sported patent leather pumps. Once more, I felt dowdy in faded blue jeans and a t-shirt that read "Hard Polka Café, Hermann, Minnesota."

"No problem." Natalie chirped. "I'll just walk with you. So, what's up? Did Bernie whack that musician or what?"

"Bernie did no such thing, Natalie. And don't you go spreading rumors either."

"Why, I would never do that, Jennifer. You know me, I'm the soul of discretion, but I heard she'd been arrested and taken off to jail. I knew something was going on when she got into that fight and now the guy turns up dead. At your booth, of all places."

"Natalie, you sure can twist things around. The deputies wanted to ask Bernie some questions. She hasn't been arrested and is now at home."

"What about the dead guy? He's the one she had the fight with, isn't he?"

" That little disagreement had nothing to do with Wes being killed. And I have no idea why whoever killed him decided to do it in the Home Arts Building."

"Maybe it was someone who has a booth there. I mean, besides you."

"Maybe whoever did it wanted to meet with him in private. It certainly didn't have anything to do with my coffee booth or me. Excuse me." I turned into the building and ignored her until she went away in a huff.

I thought of that old television show "The Honeymooners" where Jackie Gleason says to his wife, "One of these days, Alice, pow, right in the kisser." Sometimes I would love to smack Natalie.

I reluctantly stepped into the Home Arts building. I wouldn't have much time to set up before the doors opened. I didn't think we'd have much business today anyway. My nose itched when the scent of pine cleaner wafted toward me. Clicking bobbins announced

Trudy roosting on a cushioned stool in her booth. I greeted her and asked, "Who cleaned up the mess?"

"I think Frank Metzger and some of the maintenance crew got the clean-up job. Guess being Fest Meister includes some nasty duties." She chuckled as she sat flipping bobbins and making lace. "It's about time he did something useful."

"What do you mean?" I asked. "He's always hustling around here and he told me he owns a meat market. That must keep him busy."

"Being the Fest Meister is just for fun. Cleaning this place is probably the most work he's done all week. Polka Daze is his excuse to be away from the butcher shop. He never spends much time there anyway. His younger brother is half owner and Al does most of the work. Frank just stands around, looking important and shootin' the bull with folks, if he decides to show up at all."

"Well, I think he's nice. He sure helped my yesterday," I said, wondering about Trudy's attitude toward the Fest Meister.

I didn't think there would be much business today. Who'd want to go shopping where a murder had occurred? I sat down and punched "2" on my phone's speed dial to call Megan. I thought I'd call and ask her to wait to call Bernie, in case she might sleep in after meeting with Father Werner last night.

Suddenly, the doors opened and people flooded into the building. Hanging up before Megan answered, I started waiting on customers. I stayed busy for the next two hours and sold all fifty pounds of coffee.

When we got down to twelve bags of coffee, I called Sally Baumgartner and asked her to run over to Primo Gusto to roast more coffee and get over here with it. I thought people would stay away from something as gruesome as a crime scene. Instead, almost every one of my customers asked for details about the murder. Creepy.

Too Dead to Dance

When Sally finally arrived with more coffee there were still about a half dozen people waiting in line. We finally served everyone and I turned to Sally. "Thank you so much for your help. I hope I didn't take you away from anything important.

"No problem, Ms. Penny. I was just eating breakfast when you called. I didn't have any plans for today before my shift here."

"Would you mind staying a little longer? I'm starved." I asked.

"Go. Eat. I'll be fine here."

I grabbed a sausage and some hot German potato salad to eat from the brat wagon. The parents of Hermann's hockey team set up a trailer to sell bratwurst at every event in the area. Hockey is the most popular sport in Hermann and the hockey jocks are more popular than the football team, although some of the high school students play on both teams.

I called Megan, anxious to see if she got any information out of Bernie.

"I tried my best, Jennifer, but that is one stubborn woman. " She's exasperating. She kept insisting that what she knew was confidential. I don't understand. She's a nun, not a priest and a frustrating nun, too."

"Megan, you know it won't do any good to badger her. She won't change her mind and she'll get mad at us for prying. We'll have to try a different tactic to get her spill the beans."

"I don't know what else we can do. She isn't going to tell us anything."

I took a sip of my Diet Coke to wash down the brat. "No wonder the cops think she knew more than she admitted about the murdered man, she did. We need to figure a way to find out what she knows."

"Okay, Miss Detective. Where do we go from here?"

"I'm thinking, Megan. Give me a minute." I took a bite of my bratwurst. A strange breakfast at 10:30 in the morning but a better choice than the mini-donuts or deep fried cheese curds that were for sale at the food stand across from the brat wagon.

"Megan can you meet me at Primo Gusto in about an hour?"

"Sure, what for?"

"Start by roasting some more coffee, please. I'm going to need more for tonight. And while it's roasting, can you do an internet search? See what you can find out about the Windig Sangers and the people in the band."

"I can do that. I can also call a couple people who go to the local taverns where they play. I've seen them a couple times but you know how Don is about polka bands."

I had something to do here before I left the Fest Grounds. Off I went looking for Frank Metzger. I found him prancing around the big tent, to the beat of a Bavarian Two-Step. The teenaged Polka Queen and a couple Princesses followed behind him as well as a couple dozen people who popped up from the audience to join in the fun. After the music stopped for a moment, I grabbed Frank, pulled him aside, and asked him who else had keys to the Home Arts building.

"Oh, geeze, Ms. Penny, a lot of people do, the chairman of Polka Daze and the county commissioners. This is the county fairgrounds, ya know. The maintenance crew and the custodians and the groundskeepers; I think there's a key hanging in the office, too. They use the office for a first-aid station during the festival, ya know."

Great. It looked like I might be the only person in town who didn't have a key. "Is there a way to get into the building without a key?" I asked the Fest Meister, just trying to cover all the possibilities.

"Well, yah, I think so. But the cops, they already checked the windows and no one got in that way, they said. Why are you asking all these questions? You should let the sheriff's department handle this. You

Too Dead to Dance

could get hurt. Whoever killed Wes is dangerous, ya know."

"Did you know Wes?" I asked.

"Oh, yah, everyone knew Wes. He was a stinker, always getting in trouble, he was. 'Ya know, that band was up to something."

"What do you mean?"

The Fest Meister scratched his chin. "I'm not sure but something was hinky. Ray was cooking something up with Clara and Vic. I don't know what but I saw them talking together a couple of times and they always shut up when anyone came by."

"Did you tell Detective Jacobs about this?"

"Naw, what's to tell? It's just something I noticed. You be careful, Missy. You shouldn't be snooping around. You could get hurt."

"I'll be careful. Thanks for your help. Looks like the young ladies are waiting for you."

I watched him toddle back to the princesses who were now swaying to "Sierra Madre" while waving white hankies over their heads. Frank jumped right in, pulling his handkerchief from a back pocket. It must take a lot of energy to be the Fest Meister.

When I left the big tent and headed toward the parking lot, I noticed a small brick building. The sign outside proclaimed "Das Kleine Weihnachten- Geschäft" – The Little Christmas Shop.

I meandered into the building through wide double barn doors. It looked like a fairyland. Christmas lights twinkled out from behind Angel hair on a dozen Christmas trees standing around the perimeter of the room. Faux snow glittered on the tables covered with Christmas items and Polka Daze souvenirs.

The first table held hand-blown German Christmas ornaments. Fragile silver shapes were hand painted and depicted Santa, elves, stars, and Baby Jesus along with other not so Christmas figures such as a man on a motorcycle (a Harley, of course), a fisherman, Dora the Explorer, Sponge Bob, and other

Diane Morlan

whimsical characters and shapes.

The center of the table contained a bowl of hand-blown pickle ornaments painted bright green. On an attached card I read. "The Story of the Christmas Pickle." I looked around for someone to explain what a pickle had to do with Christmas when I spied wooden soldier nutcrackers wearing painted bright red uniforms, standing at attention on another table.

Next to the nutcrackers were beer steins. I checked out each one, looking for Laura's ice cream parlor stein. The first one I spied was a beautiful blue stein that had the Budweiser Clydesdales pulling a beer wagon through the snow on a starry night. I picked up a fat stein decorated with curly-cues and an Alpine Santa at the Silent Night Chapel. There was a delightful stein with a painting of the famous Nuremberg Christmas Market and hand-painted edelweiss flowers on the sides. All were beautiful. Each one was unique, but none was Coca-Cola steins.

Pen and ink sketched Christmas cards depicting scenes from around Hermann filled still another table. I saw German beer steins, shot glasses, souvenir plates, flags, cookbooks and Hummel figurines. I had never seen so many beautiful things in one place. I turned in a circle again and started feeling dizzy.

I grabbed a plastic basket and started filling it up with treasures I couldn't live without. I told myself than they were for Christmas gifts, but I knew I would keep most of them for myself. It felt good to be thinking of making my home cheerful and comfortable place to live.

I bought an armful of ornaments and other gifts to put away for Christmas, including the pickle ornament. Leaving fairyland and returning to reality, I made my way back to my coffee booth, thinking about what purchases I would give away and how many I would keep for myself. Maybe the time had come to start putting out some lovely things in my almost empty house.

Too Dead to Dance

When I arrived back at the Home Arts Building, I noticed Trudy taking a break to eat her lunch. "Trudy, can I ask you some questions about Wes?"

"I don't know much more than what I already told you, but ask away."

"What's his last name and where has he been for the past few years?

"Oh, didn't I mention his name? It's Fischer—with a "cee ach." I think he was in prison, but I don't know where or even why. I could ask Ray. He told me although Wes wasn't a great musician he needed a second chance."

"Thanks, Trudy. Don't bother Ray. I can find out what I need on the Internet."

"Oh, yah sure, the Internet. Everybody talks about the Internet. I don't know about all this new stuff. I do have a cell phone, though. I gotta admit it comes in handy some times."

I asked Sally if she could take over then said goodbye to her and Trudy. I carefully placed my precious purchases in my new folding crate and wheeled it away. I was off to meet Megan at Primo Gusto.

Diane Morlan

10

  Pulling into the parking space in front of my warehouse, I looked at the gold and black script lettering announcing "Primo Gusto Coffee Roasters" painted on the window in the door of the faded yellow building.
  I walked in and automatically did a mental check of the fifty-pound bags of raw coffee, called green beans, lining the east wall of the large room. I ordered the raw beans from a broker in Chicago and needed a few days to get my order delivered, so I did a mental count every time I came here.
  As soon as I closed the door, I could feel my shoulders relax and a sigh escaped my lips. Moving to the corner of the room, which served as my office, I saw the monitor light up Megan's face, highlighting her wild curly red hair as she hunkered over the computer.
  "Are you finding anything helpful?" I asked, pulling up a chair next to her.
  Megan shrugged and extended her arms above her head, her knit top stretching across her curvy figure. She had been wearing low-cut knit tops since she began to "bloom" in seventh grade, except at school where we wore white blouses and green plaid uniform skirts. Today's scoop-necked cotton knit summer sweater was bright green and matched her eyes. "I now

know all about the Windig Sangers Band, but not anything useful. Wes isn't even mentioned."

"I think he's the newest member of the band. His last name is Fischer. Why don't you Google him?"

While Megan tapped the keys searching for information on Wes, I went over to my shiny, new PRI-50 coffee roaster. This little beauty had become the heart of my burgeoning business.

I emptied the beans Megan had roasted and spread them out on the table to cool. Scooping raw beans out of a half filled bag, I filled a bucket with a blend of several beans we used to make our "Dunkle Starke." After weighing it, I poured seventy pounds of coffee beans into the roasting machine.

"Here we go," Megan called just as I pushed the button and the beans started roasting. "Wow. Look at this. Wes Fischer was sentenced to thirty-six months at St. Cloud Penitentiary for stalking a fourteen-year old girl. Oh, no, it says here a Catholic nun testified against him. Bernie never said a thing to me about it, did she tell you?"

I looked over my shoulder, although I knew we were alone and replied, "No, I don't know anything about it. Does it say Bernie by name?"

"No. Look, it says a Catholic nun from Hermann. That means Bernie or old Sister Dolores. She's at least ninety. Have you seen her glasses? Thick as Coke bottles. It had to be Bernie."

"Well, crap! That just makes Bernie look guiltier than ever. We need to talk to her." Walking away, I dug around in my purse that held all the things I felt I needed with me at all times. Grabbing my cell phone I told Megan, "I'm going to call her and insist we come over."

"Wait a minute, Jennifer. I just found something else. This isn't good either."

"What, more incriminating stuff about Bernie?"

"No, this is the divorce notice for Wes and his wife. It's dated two weeks after his conviction. You'll flip when you see who he was married to."

"Who? At least it can't have been Bernie."

"No, it's not Bernie. It's Martha Fischer." "Who's Martha Fisher?"

"Jennifer, what's Edwin's new girlfriend's name?" "It's Marty—Farty Marty. Oh, crap! Marty is Martha. I knew Fischer was a familiar name."

"Do you think your about-to-be-ex-husband killed his girlfriend's ex-husband?"

"Besides the fact that what you said was sort of weird, Edwin's too much of a wuss to kill anyone. He might have hid behind Marty while she did, though. Do we know anything about her? I mean, besides that she's a husband stealer."

"You can't steal what follows you home."

"I know, Megan, but it's easier to blame Marty then admitting to myself that Edwin left me for another woman."

"Buck up, Girl. You'll get through this and be the better for it." Megan leaned over and gave me a hug. I blinked fast to keep the tears at bay.

Forty minutes later, I poured fifty pounds of delicious, fragrant coffee beans across the surface of the long table. The beans Megan had roasted were now cool. As I began to package them, I enjoyed the delightful aroma of fresh roasted coffee that permeated the warehouse.

Next to the table sat an industrial sized grinder. Some of my customers prefer not to grind their own coffee, a mistake if you want a fresh, smooth cup of java. In an effort to please my customers Megan helped me grind about thirty pounds of plump, delectable coffee beans. We worked silently, while we finished packaging all the freshly roasted beans into my signature black and gold bags.

We discussed what to do about Bernie while we put the bags of coffee in boxes to tote over to the Fest Grounds. We finally decided to show up at Bernie's unannounced. If we called ahead, we'd give her time to come up with an excuse not to see us.

While shoving one-pound bags of coffee into the backseat of my Honda, a few raindrops fell on our heads. Megan and I exchanged glances over the top of the car and I said, "I hope it doesn't become a downpour or the Fest Grounds will be total muck for the Sunday parade and the final closing ceremony."

We got in and drove over to Bernie's apartment. Those few raindrops were all we saw. Not even enough to start the windshield wipers.

When St. Theresa's church converted the convent into a parish community center five years ago, Bernie and the three other nuns rented apartments near the church. Now Bernie had the distinction of being the only working nun left in town. A retired nun was living in an assisted living high-rise across town. The other two moved to a convent in South St. Paul.

Megan and I silently climbed the stairs to the second floor. Walking down the carpeted hallway to Bernie's apartment, Megan said. "What are we going to say to her?"

'I don't know. Let's just wing it. We can just tell her that we were worried about her."

We knocked on the door and it flew open as if Bernie had been waiting for us. "Thank God you're here!" She stepped into the hall, put out her arms, and enveloped us both in a bear hug.

We finally untangled and went into her tiny apartment. Walking through her miniscule kitchen in a few steps, we settled in her postage stamp sized living room. Megan and I perched on the scratchy love seat while Bernie sunk into her cushy rocking chair.

Bernie was wearing her usual uniform, but without her veil. Her short brown hair had no style. She just combed the blunt cut hair behind her ears. The only other furniture that would fit in the room was a small television set resting on an old end table I had given Bernie when she moved in here.

"The police just left. You won't believe what that

detective said to me. To me, a Catholic nun."

Megan and I looked at each other, and then I said, "Bernie, they think you killed Wes Fischer, don't they?"

"How did you figure that out? Are you the person who told that short smart-alecky detective about the dust-up I had with Wes?

As if by plan, Megan and I both got up and went to Bernie. I knelt on the floor while Megan perched on the arm of the chair.

"Of course I didn't, Bernie, but they did take you to the sheriff's department for questioning. Lots of people knew about the shouting match you had with Wes. I'm probably not the only one who figured out he's the person who let the air out of your tires. Not much stays a secret in Hermann. And Detective Decker isn't exactly short."

Megan put her hand over Bernie's hands folded in her lap. "Bernie, we need to know about the argument you had with Wes. We found out about the trial and that Wes went to jail, probably on your testimony. Tell us what happened between you two. We want to help."

Bernie sighed, crossed herself, and began talking. "It's no big deal. I didn't even recognize him; he looks so much older. Prison must have aged him. It surely did make him bitter.

"I was sitting in one of the tents, watching a group of yodeling Bavarian singers. After the performance, I got up to leave. Wes got up as I walked down the center aisle and stood in front of me. 'You lying bitch,' he hissed at me. 'If you had kept your big mouth shut I never would've gotten locked up.'"

"Oh, Bernie," I whispered. "Why was he so angry with you?"

"A few years ago, I noticed Wes pursuing a young girl after my weekly catechism class. She was really young, only about fourteen.

"The third time I spotted him, I told him to stop

slinking around the girl or I would call the police. He actually spit on my shoe! Then he said I should mind my own business.

I talked to the girl's mother, but she didn't believe the girl was in any danger. She said that Wes was a family friend. The stalking got worse with Wes camped out in front of this little girl's house.

When notes started showing up in the girl's locker at school and hang-up phone calls at home, her mother finally called the police. My testimony, along with scads of evidence convicted him in a trial that lasted only two days."

Megan said. "How awful for you. Were you frightened?"

"Not then, he was in jail. I didn't know he was out until he accosted me today. You know, he even blames me for the breakup of his marriage."

"How could that be your fault?" I asked.

"His wife, Martha came to see Fr. Werner when Wes went to jail. Fr. Werner was out of town, so Martha told me how abusive Wes had been. She didn't know if she should wait for him or not.

I told her that her she should stay away from Wes when he got out of jail, for her own safety. Of course, I couldn't advise Martha to get a divorce but I did talk to her about a legal separation and told her about the shelter for battered women she could go to if she felt unsafe. Apparently, Martha chose to go the divorce route. She served Wes with divorce papers a few months after he went to prison."

By the time she finished talking, Bernie had calmed down and granted she might need some help. "I'll pray about it and God will take care of everything."

"I'll go make some tea," Megan said, escaping to the kitchen, probably before telling Bernie that God helps those who help themselves. She's not as devout as Bernie is, but would never denigrate her beliefs.

I said, "I'm sure your prayers will be answered, Bernie. And just to make sure, Megan and I are determined to find the person responsible for killing Wes. We want to make sure your good reputation is kept intact," I said, sending up my own prayer that we could make this promise come true.

We told Bernie all we knew, which was incredibly little but when we pointed out that there were other suspects, she seemed to calm down.

"Bernie, you should also know that Martha now goes by Marty and she's living with Edwin."

"That's who Edwin is living with? She's much too young for him. Oh, my, that must be awful for you, Jennifer." She patted my hand, thinking I needed comfort. Touched by her kindness, tears came to my eyes. I squeezed her hand and thanked her.

Megan didn't have any trouble talking, though. "Bernie, we need to know who this girl is, if we're going to help you."

Bernie refused to tell us the name of the girl, even if it would put the suspicion on someone else. Megan tried to convince her it could've been the girl or one of her relatives who murdered Wes.

"You'll have to find the killer without that information, Jennifer. I promised the girl not to tell anyone who she is, when Wes went to trial. If I refused to tell Fr. Werner, you can't expect me to tell you."

On the way back to Primo Gusto, Megan let me know that regardless of what Bernie said, we needed to know more about this girl Wes had been stalking.

"You're right. Megan, I think we can find it in Bernie's office. She must have grade books from her catechism classes. We need to figure out how to get access to them.

"Jennifer! You can't burgle a church!"

"Of course not," I said grinning wickedly. "I just need a little glance at her attendance records while she's not in her office."

"We are going to burn in hell for this."

"Maybe Megan, but Bernie won't go to jail. In the meantime I need to talk to Edwin about his new little

Too Dead to Dance

sweetie."

Megan stared at me as if I had told her I needed to discuss the theory of relativity with Einstein. "Well, good luck with that.

11

When I called Edwin and asked him to meet me, he came up with one excuse after another. Finally, he agreed to meet me at a coffee shop in forty- five minutes.

I decided to use the time to check out the next place on Laura's list for the beer mug. Bavaria Haus is located on the east side of town, in a residential neighborhood. When I pulled up in front of the store, I noticed the store actually was a closed in front porch that had been singled. A sign on the door requested that bus tours call in advance. The inside of the cramped store was jam-packed with colorful items. Several shelves held packages of German food. I picked up a red tin labeled Dresdner Stollen. Next to it, a blue box indicated it held Bergen Fish Soup starter. I spied a coffee bag labeled Jacobs' Kroenung Coffee. I had to try this coffee to compare it to my own.

I picked up a green plastic shopping basket and dropped the bag of coffee into it. I passed on the chili flavored dark chocolate but grabbed two packages of Liquor-Filled - Raspberry in Orange Liqueur cookies. Megan and I would enjoy these.

The door opened and I heard a man greet the proprietor. "Marta, Honey, how are you today?"

I rounded the corner and saw a lady behind the counter. Her copper-colored hair was pulled into a sleek chignon at the nape of her neck. Al was standing in

Too Dead to Dance

front of the counter. I backed up and listened. "Oh, you sweet-talker, you. Did you bring my order?"

"Sure did, darlin'. Is there room in the cooler for it?"

"Yah, second shelf, please. Here let me sign that."

I peeked around the shelf I was hiding behind and saw Al coming through a door at the back of the store. He popped a white candy in his mouth and picked up the paper from the counter. "See you next week, Marta darling."

"Oh, you," she said, not finishing the sentence. She gave him a little punch on the arm and he turned and walked out.

"Can I help you find anything, dear?"

I jumped, and then straightened up. It was obvious that I had been eavesdropping.

"I hope so," I said, ignoring the blush I could feel creeping up my neck and warming my cheeks. Looking around the store, besides the food I saw German greeting cards, candy, and toys. One shelf held Hermann souvenirs. I handed the picture of the Coca-Cola beer stein to her.

"Oh, this is lovely. I just don't have room to carry these types of items. You might try Zunker's. They have lots of glassware."

"Thanks. They were next on my list. Oh, is that German licorice?" I picked up an envelope with a picture of a cat on it labeled "Katjes Kinder."

"Yes. Licorice cats. They're tasty if you like black licorice."

Dropping it in my basket I said, "Black is the only kind of licorice. The red stuff is just chewy candy."

Laughing, she replied, "I agree. Is there anything else I can help you with?"

"No, I'd better quit before I buy out the store."

I stuffed the large bag of groceries in the trunk and got back into my car. I popped a licorice cat in my mouth and crossed Bavaria Haus off my list. I was beginning to realize that this little favor was costing me money as well as time.

I paced in front of the counter of the Kaffee Haus, waiting for Edwin. My purse was heavy with a five-pound bag of coffee beans stuffed in it along with all my other necessities. I glanced at my watch, 2:10 PM, Edwin's favorite control technique, making me wait for him.

It had been a major deal to get him to meet with me. Cheap-o Edwin refused to pay the six-dollar entrance fee to get onto the Fest Grounds.

At first, he thought I might be trying to get him to come back to me. Fat chance of that, I had told him. When I said I wanted to discuss the divorce settlement, he decided to come right away.

Agreeing to meet me at a coffee shop that did not buy their coffee from me was another of his passive-aggressive procedures. I suppose he thought I would cave into his outrageous demands to keep all our assets. What a sap.

The top was down on his new convertible when he pulled into the parking lot. I picked up my iced vanilla latte and chocolate biscotti. Sitting down I tried to look cool and distant. Hard to do when the sweat beads almost froze to my forehead in the air-conditioned coffee shop.

Edwin sauntered in, smoothing down his windblown hair. He by-passed the coffee counter and strode over me. "I haven't got much time so let's get right to it."

What a pompous ass. I gave him my best sarcastic smile and motioned to the chair across from me. "Good to see you, too, Edwin. Please sit down."

I took a sip of coffee and almost spit it out. The licorice cat I had just eaten made the coffee taste terrible. I took a bite of biscotti to take the licorice taste from my mouth.

Edwin scraped the chair away from the table and

slapped down a manila file folder before he took a seat. "I don't have time for small talk, Jenny. I hope you are finally ready to be reasonable about the settlement."

"Don't call me Jenny." My automatic reply. "That attitude is not going to get me to sign a paper giving away everything we've worked for over the years."

"Not everything. You can have the bedroom furniture, your car, and your little coffee business. After all, I'm the one who worked for all the things I own."

"We own!" I pounded my fist on the table. "I'm the one who worked to put you through Grad school. You wouldn't be a CPA if I hadn't taught third grade to support us. Besides, I'm the one who raised our two children."

"Like raising kids is such a big deal." As usual with Edwin, I shut up and let his sarcasm roll over me.

I inhaled deeply and answered. "I guess we'll have to let the mediator help us work this out next week, okay?" "Fine, but what did you want to meet for if you're not going to sign these papers?"

"I wanted to talk to you about Marty. I think she may be in trouble."

"Marty? What are you talking about? Why don't you keep your nose out of my business?" Edwin often goes from perplexed to angry in two seconds flat. In fact, Edwin can go from any emotion to anger in a flash. His yelling is notorious among our friends and neighbors.

"Edwin, calm down and stop yelling before we get thrown out. Haven't you heard about the murder?"

"Of course I heard about it. This is Hermann. Everybody in this hick town heard about the corpse you found sprawled across your coffee stand. So, what?"

"To be precise, he was on the floor next to my booth. Don't you know who he was?"

"How would I know? I don't hang around with those kinds of people."

I bit my tongue. I tried to control my mouth. Alas, I could not help myself. I quipped, "You mean dead people?"

Before he could blow up again I added, "The man I found dead at the Fest Grounds was Wes Fischer, your girlfriend's ex-husband."

After he finished sputtering and became semi-reasonable again, I pumped him for information. "Where were you two last night? Edwin, the police will be questioning you. You need to remember the details.

"Marty and I are completely innocent. She'd never kill someone and neither would I. You know me well enough to know that, Jennifer."

"I know, Edwin, but the police don't know you. They'll want to know your whereabouts.

"I was at home all night. Marty was at the high school gym for her Jazzercise class. She got home about eleven o'clock, which was later than usual. I'm sure she stopped for coffee with friends after class. Although I've told her time and again to come straight home."

Since I didn't know the time of death, I was clueless as to whether or not Marty had an alibi. This detecting stuff was harder than I had thought. I needed more information. I needed to talk to Jacobs or Detective Decker. It might be nice to see Decker again; I would have to think about how to do that.

"You've wasted half my day, Jennifer. I'm leaving. See you at the lawyer's on Thursday."

I watched him get into his sports car and then waited for a lull in business before I went up to the teenager behind the counter.

"Is the manager in?"

"No, he won't be here for another hour. Is anything wrong?"

"Absolutely not, your service was great; however the coffee could be better." Pulling a business card out of my purse, I scribbled a note on it and handed it to the employee along with a five-pound bag of coffee. "Could you please give him this and let him know I'll call him in a few days?"

"Sure. No problem." He took the coffee and

shoved it under the counter.

As soon as I got in the car, I called Megan. I tend to do a lot of multi-tasking in the car. The traffic in Hermann is usually light so I rationalize my bad driving habits. Megan agreed we needed to find out the time of death. "I guess we also need to know the cause of death. Gee, there is so much to this investigating stuff. I had no idea it would be so difficult."

"You know, Jennifer, we don't need to know who did it, we only need to prove Bernie didn't do it."

"I don't know how to do that either. We'll have to keep plugging along and see what we can find out. Right now I need to get back to the booth and relieve Sally."

When I finally returned, Sally grabbed her tote bag and hurried out the door. "Off to class," she called over her shoulder. Darn! I had been so distracted I forgot she taught beginners swimming to a group of elementary school girls every Saturday afternoon in the summer. She must have a world of patience.

"Hi, Jennifer," Trudy called to me from her booth. "What a nice girl," Trudy nodded toward the door as Sally exited. "I was so surprised the first time she came in and started working your booth."

"You know Sally?" I asked.

"Oh, yah. She's been dating Bobby for several months. Haven't you seen her around here with him? She's at the closing ceremony every night."

"Bobby? Bobby Reinhart from your husband's band? No, I didn't know."

"Oh, yah, sure. About a month after she and Bobby started dating, Sally stopped going to any of the bands' gigs. She told Bobby something about not wanting to be a 'groupie.' I think it had something to do with Wes. When Wes tried to talk to her, she'd move away as if she hadn't heard him. After a few weeks, she started to come to our gigs again but she never did look at Wes. And Wes just kept away from her. I don't think she ever said a word to him in the three months she's been dating Bobby. They're such a cute couple."

I stood there, trying to process that information. I'd never even met Bobby but he might be trying to protect Sally. Looking at Trudy I thought, "What's wrong with this picture?"

It was too quiet. I didn't hear the clicking of bobbins coming from Trudy's booth. When I paid attention, I saw her crocheting a charming piece of lace using thread instead of yarn and a tiny silver hook. "Wow, what are you making?"

"A doily. Actually, I prefer to crochet but people like to watch me make bobbin lace so I usually do that at craft fairs. Crochet is much more relaxing."

As I watched the thread whip through her fingers, I became mesmerized. "It looks intense to me. I crochet, but only with yarn. I've made a few afghans but nothing as elegant as your doily."

"You come out to my Lace Haus and I'll teach you how to crochet with thread. The stitches are the same and you'll get used to working with thread instead of yarn. Once you get the hang of it, I know you'll love it, too."

"If you say so. I would love to learn. I'll take you up on that if I ever get any free time." We talked about when that might be while I pumped her about what she knew about Bobby, the only member of her husband's band that I had not met. I would talk to Sally later when she got back from her swim class.

"Trudy, have you heard any more about Wes' murder? I mean do they know time and cause of death?"

'I haven't heard anything about when but I sure know how."

"What do you mean?" I asked, puzzled by this remark.

She reached into a canvas tote bag and held up a long red knitting needle. "Why, Jennifer, didn't you see my other number ten sticking out of his neck?"

Confused, I asked inanely, "You knit, too?"

"Yah, and I feel sort of bad about leaving my needles out on in the open." Trudy said, ignoring my

Too Dead to Dance

perplexity. "I was trying to finish a scarf before closing. I got the last row bound off just as everyone was leaving and the Fest Meister was waiting to lock up. I tucked the scarf in my tote bag, but left the needles on the table."

I had been so shocked at seeing a dead body I hadn't looked at the details. Trudy was much more observant, but, after all, it was her knitting needle. When she showed me its twin, I understood how I could have missed it, a red aluminum needle about a foot long with a pointed end.

It occurred to me that the killer had not planned to kill Wes or he would have brought a weapon. From what I had heard today, plenty of people had reason to do away with the scoundrel. Somehow, I needed to figure out who actually followed through.

When Sally returned from teaching her class, she had barely put down her bag when we had a rush of customers, so I didn't get a chance to talk to her. The booth stayed busy until almost seven o'clock when Sally's shift ended. After Sally left, I took a minute to call Megan. We needed to make a plan.

I told Megan about Trudy's knitting needle being the murder weapon and she agreed that the murder probably wasn't planned.

"You know, Jennifer, you need to talk to Marty. Edwin won't be any help there so you also need to find a way to get to her when Edwin's not around."

"Let me think about how to do that. Tonight I plan to find Sally at the big tent while she's watching the Windig Sangers and find out what she knows about Wes. I don't even know the time Wes was attacked. I guess we'd better find that out first or nobody's alibi will make any sense. How do I do that?"

Megan suggested, "Why don't you drop in at Maron County Sheriff's Department and see if Lt. Jacobs would tell you the details. He probably won't, but you can't receive if you don't ask."

"Good idea. I'll drop in when I leave here tonight.

What are you doing tonight? Want to go with me?"

"I'd love to, but I'm waiting for a call from Don. I think he's out west somewhere. Las Vegas, Los Angeles, some Las-town."

"Okay, I'll call you tomorrow after I go to church." "Don't get caught breaking into Bernie's office. I still think you're nuts."

"Well, Bernie won't have me locked up, but I'll be careful. See you tomorrow."

I closed up the coffee booth around eight o'clock, an hour before the building closed. It was Saturday night and the Fest Grounds were filled with young adults who wanted beer, not coffee. I gathered up the bags from the Christmas Shop and made my way through the throng of young people to the parking lot.

The red brick building that housed the sheriff's office, jail, and county court rooms and offices sat in the center of town. An old cannon graced the park-like yard in front of the building. I pulled into the parking lot at the side of the building and climbed the steep stairs of the main entrance, wondering whatever happened to accessibility. I grabbed the door handle but before I could pull it open, it flew outward, almost knocking me over.

"Watch it!" I shouted.

"Ohmygod, I'm sorry. Are you okay?" Detective Decker grabbed me and held me as I tilted backward toward the steps.

I began to yell at him when I remembered why I wanted to talk to him. "Detective Decker, I'm okay. You can let me go now."

He smiled down at me but kept one beefy arm around my not so tiny waist. "Can I help you?"

"Well, actually, you know, I have a question for you, I mean ..." Good grief, what happened to my college education? I sounded like an idiot. I told myself to get a grip.

His concern turned to amusement and when he

grinned down at me, I grabbed his arm and flung it away. "Detective Jecker, I mean Decker, did you find out the time of death?"

"Whose death? What are you talking about?"

"How many murders are you investigating? This is the first one here in years. I'm talking about Wes Fischer."

"Did you know Fischer?" He asked while avoiding my question.

"Not while he was alive, but you guys are trying to pin this on my friend and I need to know when he was killed."

"Playing Jessica Fletcher, Ms. Penny?"

"It's Jennifer," I replied, thinking he could've said Nancy Drew. Did he have to pick the oldest mystery sleuth besides Miss Marple? "I would like to know if I might have been with Bernie when someone else killed Wes. Unlike you, I know she didn't do this."

"You may be a good friend, but that doesn't make her innocent. Were you with her between midnight and 3 A.M.?"

"No," I said. "I was home tucked in bed."

"Alone?" he asked that smirky grin back on his gorgeous face.

I pretended not to hear the question. "Did your Crime Scene people get any DNA?"

Decker chuckled and then he answered me. "Jennifer, you watch too much television. It takes five to ten days to get DNA identification. That is, once the lab techs get to it. The backlog at the Minnesota Crime Bureau Lab is about three months right now. And what would we do with the results once we get them? We have to connect them to a suspect. Think Sr. Bernadine will let us swab her cheek?"

"I don't know," I sputtered. "What about fingerprints? They would show that Sr. Bernadine wasn't even in that building."

"Could be, but, there were thousands of fingerprints in that building. Even if we had some specific prints, we can't stick them in a scanner and have the computer spit out the killer's name and picture in thirty seconds. It just doesn't work that way."

"This is so frustrating." I stamped my foot and turned to leave.

"Jennifer, be careful," he said, hands on hips. "This isn't a game. There is a murderer out there. You could be in danger playing detective."

"I'm not playing at anything. I'm just asking a few questions."

"If you find out anything important, you need to tell me. Don't put yourself in jeopardy." He actually sounded concerned.

Too Dead to Dance

12

I used my expert multi-tasking skills to I back out of the parking space, call Megan and, when I had the car headed back to the Fest Grounds, write the time of death in my new little notebook while steering the Honda with my leg.

"Megan, why is he acting so concerned about my safety?"

"Maybe he isn't acting. It's apparent he's as attracted to you as you are to him."

"This is getting so complicated. I don't have time for this right now. I need to concentrate on getting Bernie out of trouble."

"Your mind might be telling you that, but your heart and some other parts of your body are trying to convince you of something else."

I groaned, shaking my head in an effort to get my mind back on the problem. On Thursday night, Polka Daze had closed up at eleven o'clock. There would be no witnesses at a deserted Fest Grounds between midnight and three o'clock in the morning. Trudy might have noticed if Wes left alone or with anyone after the closing ceremony. I'd ask her later.

Right now, I headed over to Primo Gusto to roast extra coffee for tomorrow. On the last day of Polka Fest, vendors always had a brisk business with the out -of- towners picking up items they had been looking at all weekend. I needed to email an order to my supplier for several different coffee beans. Business had been better this weekend than any other festival where I had set up

Too Dead to Dance

shop. All this activity because of Wes' murder. How gruesome.

It was late when I finished roasting, cooling, and bagging the coffee and was almost eleven o'clock by the time I pulled into the Fest Grounds' parking lot.

The big tent overflowed with people of all ages. There were at least eighty picnic tables plus the bleachers in the back of the tent, all filled with revelers. Over a thousand people enjoyed the music on this sweltering, muggy Saturday night in July. Three colossal barn fans moved the air around but it didn't feel like it helped much. Drinking beer and a lot of it seemed to be the way people were coping with the heat.

Some of the young guys at one table had built a pyramid with upside-down plastic beer cups. I stopped to look at the tall plastic edifice. One kid reached up to put another beer cup on top and the whole structure tumbled down on their heads. They laughed uproariously in total disregard of the time and effort it had taken to build it.

Young women in dirndls wove through the crowd with palettes of plastic shot glasses, selling schnapps for a dollar. The band on stage played "Edelweiss" while the whole crowd swayed to the music holding beer glasses above their heads.

By this time of night most of the music included audience participation. As soon as the song ended, the singers sat down and the band started up with the "Chicken Dance." People swarmed to the aisle, flapping their arms and clucking.

Laughing, I pressed through the crowd to the beer wagon and ordered a berry wine cooler. It took forever to get through the crowd to the picnic table next to the stage where Trudy, Sally and several other women sat. They shouted a greeting over the loud music and moved together to make room for me to sit down.

One of the women plopped a funnel cake covered in powered sugar on the table. The merrymakers dived into it. I couldn't believe these people were eating sweet funnel cake and drinking beer. You gotta love those Germans.

A pretty girl wearing a dirndl and blonde braids sauntered up to our table. She held out a board that had little holes in it. Plastic shot glasses were nestled in the holes. "Root beer shots, anyone? Only one ticket."

I threw out three tickets and bought one for Trudy, Sally and me. Sally downed hers while Trudy and I sipped ours.

When the next song began, we watched Frank, the Fest Meister, and the Polka Princesses marching through the tent, grabbing up people and making a long snaky line. Then the Fest Meister and the Polka Queen turned, joined hands and made a bridge for the marchers to go under. As soon as they cleared the bridge, they turned and put up their hands until all the participants had gone under. Then they turned and marched back through the crowd.

I thought I heard Trudy whisper. "Smarty pants." "Did you say something, Trudy?" I asked.

"No. Well, ya, I did," she said turning to me. "That Frank thinks he's so important,"

"Why don't you like him?" I asked.

Trudy pulled herself up and said, "I'll tell you why. About five years ago, he quit his perfectly good job at the pizza factory and got his brother to quit his job at Stanley's Supermarket. They put all their savings into that meat market.

Frank was such a penny-pincher that Ida, his wife took a part-time job. She told a friend of mine that she just wanted to be able to buy some new clothes. Then Ida died right before they bought the meat market. I think she was just worn out. He thinks he's better than everyone else is. He's been that way since high school."

"Their business is successful, isn't it?"

"Well, yah, because of Al. I think he does most of the work. I think Frank used Ida's life insurance to buy his share of the meat market. I just don't like him."

"I don't know, Trudy. His private life is his business. I think he's nice. And he sure is a great Fest Meister."

I finished my schnapps, feeling weird drinking from a small plastic cup like those used at church for Communion wine.

"Who is taking Wes' place in the band, Trudy?" I hadn't realized until now that Wes' death left the band short one musician.

"For now we just have people from other bands filling in when they can. Before Wes joined the band, a girl from Itzeg played the trumpet. But she got pregnant and had to quit. She said for every pound she gained she lost more breath. Couldn't do the riffs anymore." Trudy laughed and stuck a piece of funnel cake in her mouth and washed it down with her beer. "The young ones, they come and go. Ray said without Clara and Vic, the band would had never lasted this long. But we keep finding new talent and it helps the young ones get some experience, too."

During the break between the last band and the grand finale, I asked Trudy about Thursday night. "Did you see Wes talking to anyone after their set?"

"No, not anyone special. Some girls always talk to the younger guys. Of course the Fest Meister and one of the Princesses were talking to him during one of the breaks."

She tapped her finger on her chin. "You know, I remember there was someone. This good-looking lady talked to him during one of the breaks towards the end of the evening. Must have been around ten-thirty. A tall woman, with amazing reddish-brown hair. Long, thick hair, past her shoulders. They were intense and Wes kept shaking his head and grinning at her. Then she stomped her foot, turned, and marched out of the tent."

My mouth dropped open. I was too stunned to speak. Trudy had described Marty. Edwin said she got in about eleven but did she leave later to confront Wes? Why? Did he have something on her? Did she want something from him? Shoot, the more questions I ask the more questions that came up. I would never get this figured out.

I sat there thinking for a while before I became conscious of the fact that I had been munching on funnel cake and drinking my wine cooler. It was sort of a tasty combination. Who knew?

I attempted to brush powered sugar off the front of my shirt and slid over closer to Sally, thinking I could talk to her.

Just then, a tall, lanky man threw a leg over the picnic table between Trudy and me. Straddling the picnic table bench he said, "Hey, ladies, I'm here. Have you been waiting long?"

The ladies at the table laughed and, believe it or not, Trudy actually blushed. The lady who had bought the funnel cake just frowned then turned her attention toward the bandstand and ignored all of us.

He pulled his other leg over and deposited his beer bottle on the table. "Has anyone seen my brother?" He asked.

Trudy said, looking around, "He was just here. Over there with the Princesses. I wonder where he went."

One of the ladies at the table said, "He might have gone to another tent. The Hermann Minnesangers are performing at the next tent right now. Maybe he wanted to hear them."

"He's only heard them most of his life," remarked Trudy.

Grinning at me, the sandy-haired man said, "Hi, I'm Al. Hey, didn't I almost run over you the other day?"

"Watch out, Jennifer, he's a heart breaker," Trudy warned me.

"Don't believe a word she says," Al replied. "She's secretly in love with me, but don't tell Ray."

Everyone at the table laughed then went back to watching the bands on stage. I shook my head while checking out this attractive guy with light green eyes and tousled blonde hair. He flashed me an alluring smile.

"Yes," I replied, "I'm the one who fell in front of your truck. Thanks for helping me pick up my coffee bags."

"No, problem. I've been waiting for a beautiful woman to fall for me."

"That is the most pitiful pick -up line I've ever heard. Aren't you going to ask me what my sign is?"

"Naw, don't need to. I know we're compatible." Without that smile, he never would've gotten away with such silly lines, but he was so cute all I could do was laugh.

"Ah, Jennifer," Al said, holding my left hand between his, probably checking to see if I was wearing a wedding ring. "Lover of peace."

"What? How do you know what my name means?"

"I know all sorts of things, Jennifer. I know I'd like to go out with you. Can I have your number? Can I call you?" A hank of hair fell over his forehead as he flashed that grinned at me again.

I felt my throat constrict. I hadn't been asked out since college. My nervous laugh was a wee bit shrill as I squeaked out an answer. "Jennifer Penny. I'm in the book."

He kissed the back of my hand and then stood up, bowed at the waist and said, "'Til we meet again." He grabbed his bottle of Leinenkugel and melted into the crowd.

"Wow! What was that all about?" I asked Trudy. "Oh, that's just Al. He's harmless. Well, to us married ladies. You'd better watch out though. He loves the ladies. He has a whole bevy of women who are in and out of the meat market all day."

"Maybe that's why his business is successful," I said, laughing. "He flirts with them and they buy pot roasts just to see him. Pretty simple business plan."

"I think he does more than flirt, Jennifer," Trudy

warned me. "He's a real ladies man."

"It doesn't matter. I'm not even divorced yet and I'm certainly not interested in getting involved with any man for a long time—if ever."

"Yah, sure. I've heard that before," Trudy the Sage replied, picking up her cup and draining the last of her beer.

She was probably right. First gorgeous Detective Decker, now this fine-looking guy. Maybe being single wasn't so bad after all. Jennifer, stop! I told myself. You do not want to go there. And I didn't come here to flirt with men or try to figure out my life. I was here to help Bernie.

"I don't mean to eavesdrop," said the lady who had bought the funnel cake. "But Wes and Al didn't get along when they were kids."

"They didn't?" Trudy and I both replied at once. "Man, they were always at each other. In high school Wes made the varsity football team but Al was just a second stringer, a bench warmer. When Wes got kicked out of school for having drugs in his locker, Al got moved up. We all figured that Al ratted out Wes or maybe even planted the dope."

"You went to high school with Wes and Al?" I asked. "Yeah, I'm Della. Della Younger."

"Younger? Are you related to Natalie?" "Unfortunately, she's my aunt. My dad is her older brother. How do you know her? Not that anyone in town doesn't know her."

"We went to St. Theresa's together, first through eighth grade. Were you in the same class as Wes and Al?"

"No, I was a year behind them. I dated Al when I was in tenth grade. We broke up because he couldn't keep his eyes and hands off the other girls in school. I dated Wes in my junior year. He was already out of school. I didn't go with him for long. He was really possessive and besides he got into trouble all the time. My folks were having a fit about me going with a guy who was on probation. When my mom heard about Wes being killed, she said that he probably got what he deserved. Not very sympathetic, my mom."

"Do you think that Al could've killed Wes?" I asked. "Why? I doubt they've even spoken to each other in years. Wes just got out of jail. Besides, didn't that nun kill him?"

"No, she didn't." I bristled. "I've known Sister Bernadine most of my life. She could never hurt another human being."

"Whoa, sorry. I'm just saying what I heard," Della put up her hands in defense.

"Oh, I know. I'm just so tired of everyone talking about her." I patted Della on the arm and thanked her for the information.

I turned to Sally to ask her about Wes and Bobby but she shushed me when the music started and the closing ceremony began.

The mood changed from merry to solemn. Each band played the National Anthem of the country they represented. There were German bands of course, but also Austrian, Tyrolean, Swiss, and several other bands from small countries in Europe. Even the Canadians came down for the celebration.

When the Windig Sangers and a couple other American bands started the National Anthem, the entire audience stood with hand over heart and sang along. By the time we got to "home of the brave," all the revelers at our table had tears on their cheeks.

Mellowed out from the schnapps, wine cooler and a few bites of funnel cake for supper, I slid down the picnic table bench to talk to Sally. Just then, she jumped up and headed for the back of the stage. A young man with a boyish grin came down the steps, flipped open a cooler and took out a long necked bottle of Leinenkugel beer. He popped it open, took a big swig, and then grabbed Sally, spinning her around in a circle. I recognized Bobby from yesterday when Jacobs was questioning him.

They were laughing, their noses touching when I got up to make my way out of the tent along with about eight hundred other fest-goers.

When I finally made my way through the crowded exit, I strolled along the roadway toward the parking lot. Metzger's meat truck made its way through the Fest Grounds. Under the streetlight, I saw Al and sitting next to him was a blonde I recognized as one of the Polka Princesses. A little young for him, I thought. Why do men always seem to chase after the young ones, I pondered.

I peeked into the mid-sized tent. There was a band onstage playing, of all things, country music. This must be the German band from Texas. I listened for a while looking over the crowd. I spied Natalie Younger sitting with a group at a ringside table. Everyone was drinking draft beer from plastic keg cups, except Natalie. She poured her beer into two keg cups from a bottle of Leinenkugel.

What was with people drinking Wisconsin beer? They must have brought it with them because the only beer sold here was Schueller beer, brewed right here in Hermann. She handed one of the cups of beer to the man next to her. His back was to me so I couldn't see who it was. A man in lederhosen with salt and pepper grey hair. It might be the Fest Meister but from the back, it also looked like half the men here at Polka Daze.

Too tired to call Megan, I went over things in my head on my way home. Why did Marty come to the Fest Grounds Thursday night? What about Al? He kept turning up everywhere. Sally didn't want anything to do with Wes. Why? I wanted to call Detective Decker but what would I say? That Sally didn't like Wes? That's not a motive. Maybe I just wanted to talk to the sexy detective. Not paying attention as I drove down the empty street, I daydreamed about Detective Decker and his delicious mouth.

A dark vehicle pulled up next to me. Thinking it

wanted to pass; I slowed and pulled a little to the right.

As the vehicle came abreast of my car, it swerved closer to my front fender. I moved over more, barely staying on the pavement. It moved in closer. I hit the brakes and twisted the wheel to the right. My Honda shot up the curb. I braked to a stop at the foot of a massive old Sugar Maple. My head lurched back, hit the headrest, and then bounced forward. I heard something in my neck pop.

By the time I caught my breath and looked for the vehicle that had forced me off the road, all I could see were two red dots disappearing around a curve.

I dug in my leather purse for my cell phone and called 9-1-1. Again.

13

When a Hermann police officer arrived, she took notes while I told her I thought it was a truck, van, or SUV that had run me off the road. "I don't know the color but it was dark and larger than a car."

"Have you been drinking?" She asked.

"I was at Polka Daze. I had a wine cooler."

"Just one?" She raised an eyebrow, my signal that she didn't believe me.

"Actually, I also had a schnapps shot. And some funnel cake."

"Okay. Let me get the breathalyzer and check you out. Just for the record."

The breathalyzer was painless but embarrassing. She told me the number, but it didn't mean a thing to me. "You're fine. You passed," she said.

Thank goodness for that. All I needed was to have to call Megan to bail me out of jail.

We both turned as a shiny Dodge Ram with a flashing light stuck at an angle to the roof came to a screeching halt behind the cruiser. Detective Decker jumped out and grabbed me by the shoulders. "Are you hurt? Do you need an ambulance? Who did this?"

"I don't know, no, and I don't know. What are you doing here?"

He stuck his thick hands in the pockets of his tight jeans and kicked a pebble with his shoe. I noticed he wore a wrinkled t- shirt and no socks. "I was listening to the police scanner at home and heard your name." His head came up and he scolded me. "I told you to be careful and now look what happened."

"Hey, I was just driving home from Polka Fest. Don't get all parental on me." I shot him a look that told him to shut up.

I repeated the whole story again for his benefit. "Now will you help me get my car back on the road?"

"Why don't you let me take you over to the hospital and have a doctor check you out?"

"I'm fine. All I need is a hot shower and a good night's sleep."

Detective Decker gave me that smirky grin again but didn't suggest that he help me with those chores. "It doesn't appear your car is damaged but you might want to have it checked out tomorrow. I can't believe the air bags didn't go off."

I thanked the police officer, waved at Decker, and drove away. In my rear view mirror, I saw Decker pull out behind me. He followed me all the way home. When I turned into my driveway, he cruised up behind my Honda and got out of his truck.

"Sorry I yelled at you before."

"Oh, that's okay. I've been married, I'm used to it," I said, trying to sound cute.

"I hope it hasn't turned you against all men. I worry about you."

"Why?" I asked. "You don't even know me."

He grabbed my shoulders again, this time more gently. "I'd like to. Can we have dinner soon and start to get to know each other?"

Dinner? What's with all these dinner invitations? I sure didn't look like a needed a meal.

It looked like Megan had been right. He was attracted to me. Well, how about that, I thought. I almost laughed aloud and then remembered Bernie.

"I can't. You think my friend killed Wes and I know she didn't. You won't even look anywhere else."

"What makes you think we aren't looking at anyone else? Did I ever tell you that?"

No, he hadn't. I just assumed they were going to pin this on Bernie and I was the White Knight who would need to come to her rescue.

"Who else are you looking at? Why didn't you tell me this before?"

"You seem to like to jump to conclusions," he said, a smug look on his pleasing face. "What makes you think I can share confidential information with you?"

"Fine. Don't tell me. I'll keep looking for myself." I turned to walk away when he grabbed my arm and swung me around.

"You are an exasperating woman. I can't tell you anything about an open case. I can tell you that you're right or wrong if you ask me about something in particular."

"You're just trying to find out what I know. Okay, ask my about-to-be-ex-husband what his new girlfriend was doing talking to Wes, her ex-husband, by the way, on the night he was killed."

Good grief, I had begun to sound like Natalie Younger.

"Marty Fischer was at Polka Fest the night Wes was killed? Guess we'll have to have another talk with her."

So, they had been looking for other suspects. Good, but it still didn't take Bernie off the hook.

"Give me your cell phone," he said.

"What for?" I asked, digging in my purse for it.

He took my phone and punched in some numbers. "If you need me just push 'four' and 'talk'."

I took back the phone he handed to me. About to say something about a donut run, I decided, for once, to keep my mouth shut.

"Okay, now will you go out with me?" Jerry asked. "Not until we find out who Wes Fischer's real killer is and you admit Sister Bernadine is innocent."

Jerry stuck his hands in his pockets again and looked me right in the eyes. "I'll hold you to that," he said. He turned and walked away, wiggling his fingers over his shoulder. Nice broad shoulder. Nice butt, too.

Then I ran the conversation through my head again, I deduced that the deputies had talked to Marty. And she'd lied to them about being at Polka Fest. Maybe she didn't lie. Maybe she omitted information that would make her look guilty.

The detectives might talk to her again but I needed to know what she had to say. The cops sure weren't going to tell me anything. And I still had to get a look at Bernie's grade book and talk to Sally.

Thank goodness, I had organized my coffee roasting schedule to delegate the roasting to several college students. I hired three students to come in on the weekends to help me do the roasting. Each Friday I put up a schedule that notes when and how much coffee we need each day for the following week.

It also notes where the coffee will go, for restaurants and other establishments that buy my coffee, as well as the fairs and festivals I attend. The students make sure there is enough coffee roasted and bagged to meet the demand. It worked out surprisingly well. Unless, like today, there is more demand than usual.

I had arranged for Sally to take the first shift so she would open the booth at Polka Daze tomorrow morning. That would give me time to snoop around Bernie's office. I knew she would be at Mass from seven to eight o'clock.

When I pulled off my shirt, I noticed powered sugar sprinkled over the front. Good grief, Detective Decker must think I'm a slob, I thought. Maybe it hadn't shown up in the dark. I grabbed an icepack from the freezer, pressed it to the back of my neck and climbed into bed. Tonight I was wearing a silky chemise I had dug out of a box in my closet this morning. I set my alarm, again thinking about Jerry Decker while I drifted off to sleep.

Diane Morlan

14

Sunday

I swallowed a couple ibuprofen caplets before getting out of my car in front of St. Theresa's Catholic Church, greeting several people I knew attending the ten o'clock Mass this Sunday morning. While the others went straight into the nave, I took a sharp right turn, grabbed a bulletin, and glanced over it as I headed down the stairs, looking for the classroom where Bernie and her volunteers teach catechism classes on Saturday mornings.

I had planned to be here while Bernie attended the seven o'clock Mass. It would have been much easier to sneak into her office while she was upstairs, but my neck hurt so bad when I woke up that I took some ibuprofen and went back to sleep.

Oh, crap. An announcement in the bulletin stated that Bernie would be teaching a special class for the next several weeks during the ten o'clock Mass for the second graders who were studying for their First Communion.

Now I had to sneak around the church basement while Bernie taught a group of second graders in the classroom next to her office.

When I came upon a solid door labeled "Sister Bernadine Lenhert, Director, CCD," I looked both ways, then listened for Bernie.

Too Dead to Dance

"Okay, children, settle down. Let's start with an easy question. What is Holy Eucharist?"

"I know, I know, I know. Pick me, Sister."

"Alright, Patrick. Tell us what the Holy Eucharist is."

"It's communion! See I know."

"Yes, its communion, Josh, but it's also a sacrament. So, class, what is a sacrament? Mary?"

"It's something Jesus gave us to get grace." "Right, Mary. Do you know what grace is?" "Yep. She's my auntie."

Okay, those kids were going to keep her busy for a while. I slowly turned the knob on the office door. Knowing Bernie's trusting manner, I guessed the door wouldn't be locked. It slid open soundlessly. I slipped into the room, closed the door, leaned against it and began to breathe again.

A trickle of sweat ran down my cheek and not from the morning heat. The only source of light in this crowded little room came from a small window set high on the outside wall. I didn't dare turn on the lights. Although there was no window in the door, light might seep out under the door and give me away. I gazed around the closet-sized room.

It was a tight fit for the chair between the desk and the wall. Bernie might be skinny enough to fit there but I could only stand next to the desk and reach over. I yanked the drawer handle, almost jerking my arm out of the socket. A throbbing pain snaked up my neck. The ice pack I had put on my neck after the car accident last night hadn't helped much. The door was locked. Damn. Oops. Guess I shouldn't be cursing in church.

Bernie's attempt at security was pitiful. I opened the center drawer of her desk, reached way in the back until I felt the keys. I drew them out and opened my hand. On a red carabineer hung an "O" ring with two keys. The larger key had a tag marked "Supply Cabinet" in Bernie's neat script. I grinned, looking at the small key, labeled "File Cabinet."

Footsteps echoed down the hall. I stood stock-still, my breath caught in my throat. They tapped right past the office door without hesitating. I let out a sigh and as I turned to go back to the file cabinet, I dropped the keys.

Down on my hands and knees, I searched under the desk, squeezing between the desk and wall and over the chair legs. The area under the desk was as dark as pitch. I couldn't see anything. I kept feeling around until my hand finally touched the metal. I grabbed them and got up, wondering why I couldn't see the bright carabineer under the desk.

I opened the top file drawer, then went over to the door and opened it a crack. I listened for Bernie, to make sure I was still safe in here.

"How many sacraments are there?" Bernie asked. I heard Benny's voice shout, "A whole bunch!"

I shut the door and riffled through folders until I found a thick file labeled "CCD Class Attendance Records." Pulling out the Teacher's Roll Book for the year of Wes' arrest, I began to run my finger down the list of eighth and ninth graders. I heard a toilet flush and footsteps came my way again. Two girls giggled and whispered as they walked past the office door. I stood stock-still. This fear couldn't be good for my heart.

When the footsteps faded, I held the book up toward the little window and quickly scanned the attendance record. I gasped when I came to the second name on the ninth grade list—Baumgartner, Sally.

That explained Sally's attitude toward Wes. Even so, it made Bernie look even more suspicious. Being fearless, Bernie wouldn't hesitate to confront him and tell him off. Could things have gone wrong while she was trying to protect Sally? No, I refused to believe Bernie could do something like this, but could Sally? I sure would like to find a suspect I didn't like. Like Marty.

Putting the book back in the folder, I locked the file cabinet. I pulled the desk drawer open and shoved the keys toward the back. Tiptoeing to the door, I opened it an inch and peeked out into the hall, looking for someone waiting to catch me. All clear.

"Very good class. You're learning, but you have to study this week. First Communion is in eight weeks and you have to know the answers to these questions."

I dashed down the hallway. My shoes tapped on the steps as I ran up the stairway. When I reached the top, I turned toward the music and knelt down in the back pew. I needed some divine guidance with this problem.

I left Mass before the final blessing. I needed to get an ice pack on my neck. I had just closed the door behind me when I heard my name.

"Why Jennifer, I'm so glad to see you at Mass. Did you leave early?"

Oh, crap, busted. "Hi, Bernie. Yes, I had a little accident last night and my neck hurts. I need an ice pack." I always think it's best to lie as close to the truth as possible.

"Jennifer, what happened? Can I help?"

"No, no. I'm fine. I got run off the road last night on my way home from the Fest Grounds after the closing ceremony. I really am fine."

"I thought the Home Arts building closed at nine o'clock? Why were you there so late? Were you out festing with Megan?"

"No, I just wanted to talk to a few people about … stuff."

"Jennifer, are you sticking your nose into this investigation? Didn't the police tell you to stay out of their way?"

"Yes, and so did you, but I can't sit around and watch the cops haul you off to jail. I have to do what I can to help."

"You can best help by keeping your nose out of this. It will all work out. I'm sure no one really believes that I could kill someone. For heaven's sake, Jennifer. I'm a nun!"

"I know. I said the same thing to the cops. A lot of good that did."

"Just let it be, Jennifer. There are things that don't need to come out. Things that could hurt innocent people."

"Bernie, I'll do my best to keep from hurting anyone but you have to know that I'm willing do whatever it takes to prove that you're innocent."

"You may be willing, Jennifer, but you don't know how much some of the things you do hurt other people. Please stay out of this. You're not the police. It's not your job to prove anything."

I gave up, said goodbye and walked to my Honda. I'd just have to try to stay out of her way until this was over. I hated lying to Bernie. Not just because she was a nun, but also because she was one of my best friends.

When I got to my Honda, I noticed the bags from the Christmas Shop in the back seat. I'd try to remember to take them in the next time I stopped at my townhouse.

Before I went over to the Fest Grounds, I decided to stop at Glessner's German Store. I knew they would be open on Sunday, because of Polka Daze.

Glessner's was exactly the opposite of Bavarian Haus. Roomy floor space with open tall display towers spaced so it was easy to move between them around the store. The glass shelves held Hummel figurines, clear glass plates, platters, vases, and decanters.

The inside wall of the store was completely filled with German nutcrackers. Signs near each section indicated the manufacturer: Ulbricht, Steinbach, KWO, and others. Each company had its own unique style. Some nutcrackers reflected professions: fireman, doctor, cowboys. Others showcased nationalities: Irish, Swiss, even a Native American.

I picked up a wooden figurine of a Policeman. It was made by Steinbach, but wasn't a nutcracker. Looking close I saw that it was an incense burner. Next to it was an aviator incense burner. I made a mental note; if Megan and Don were still together next December, I'd get the cute little pilot incense burner for her Christmas gift.

I found a display case that held beer glasses and steins. Pilsner, wine, and highball glasses, as well as clear glass beer mugs. The bottom two shelves held steins with intricate designs including wildlife, military, and city scenes. No Coca-Cola stein.

On a low built-in counter under the nutcrackers were more Hermann souvenirs and an array of German chocolate candy. I pulled myself away and went to the counter. I knew Mr. Glessner. This wasn't my first time in this store. As usual, it was again a delightful experience.

"Mr. Glessner, do you carry this stein?" I asked handing him the picture.

"It's a very nice piece, but, I wouldn't carry this here."

"Why not?"

"Because it was made in Brazil, not Germany. Almost everything in here is made in Germany."

"Brazil? Why would Brazilian's make beer steins?"

"There are lots of Germans in South America. I don't carry beer steins made in the United States either, just Germany."

"Do you know where I might find one of these steins?"

"Have you tried the Internet? You might find one on eBay."

"I already tried that. Thanks, anyway."

Back in my car, crossing another store off my list, I wondered if Laura even wanted this stein if it wasn't made in Germany. I don't know where Laura had seen this stein, but I was beginning to doubt that it was here in Hermann.

I pulled my cell phone out of my purse and found Biergarten Restaurant in my contacts list. I hit the button and a few seconds later Laura picked up her phone.

"Biergarten Restaurant, Laura speaking. May I help you?"

"Hi, Laura. It's Jennifer."

"Jennifer! Did you find my beer stein?"

"No I haven't but I did find out that it was made in Brazil, not Germany. I just wanted to check and see if you still want it."

"Of course I want it. I don't care where it was made or even when. I just want it."

"Well, I wasn't sure so I thought I'd better check." "Thanks, Jennifer, but my steins aren't all from Germany. They came from all over the world. I just buy the ones I like."

Okay, so the steak and lobster dinner was still a possibility. I would keep looking. "Okay, Laura. I'll check out the rest of the places on my list. I'll call you when I find it."

"There's no hurry, Jennifer. I know you're busy with Polka Daze. Just look for it when you're near the places I listed. I don't want you to go to too much trouble over this. It's not that important."

"It's no problem, Laura," I lied. "Actually, I'm enjoying the stores I've been to." This was true. "I'm on a mission now. I will find the stein."

I put the car in reverse and turned to look out the back window. When someone tapped on my window and called my name, I almost jumped out of my skin.

"Jennifer! Jennifer! Open the window!" Natalie Younger was tapping away on my window. Just what I needed to make my day complete.

I rolled down the window about two inches and said, "I can't talk right now, Natalie. I'm in a hurry. I have to get to the Fest Grounds."

"Just tell me what's going on, Jennifer. Did Bernie get arrested? Did she whack that guy?"

I hit the button and rolled up the window then slowly backed out of the parking space. Natalie was still asking me questions when I waved at her and drove away.

On the way to the Fest Grounds, I called Mark Jensen, one of the college students who worked for me and asked him to meet me at the coffee booth. It would be a busy day and I needed extra help to be able to move around and not leave Sally to do all the work. As soon as Mark arrived, I grabbed Sally's hand and I led her out of the Home Arts Building. We went around the corner of the building to a picnic table where we could sit and talk in some semblance of privacy.

"Do you know my friend, Sister Bernadine, Sally?" Sally picked at a thread on her vest. "Of course I know her. I belong to St. Theresa's. She taught my Catechism class."

"Do you know that the police suspect that she killed Wes?"

"They can't really believe that. Sister Bernadine wouldn't hurt a fly."

"I know. And I'm trying to prove that she's innocent. But I need your help."

"How can I help? I wasn't even here when his body was found, you were.

"That's right, but I have some information that I need cleared up. Sally, I know this won't be easy for you but I need to know how you met West."

"I don't like to talk about that. It's sad and embarrassing."

I leaned in closer and put my arm on her shoulder. "I know about your father, Sally. It's okay, I understand."

Sally, took a deep breath, squared her shoulders, and said, "Wes was a friend of my father's. Dad was killed during a bank robbery. After that, Wes started coming around our house almost every day, usually about the time I got home from school. I was just a kid and the way he looked at me kind of gave me the creeps." She shuddered.

"Did you tell your mother how you felt?" I asked. "Sure, but she said I was being silly, that Wes just wanted to be nice to us. I was so angry that my father had been shot. I even got mad at my mother for sticking up for Wes. I was mad at the world for a while."

"Did your mother finally do something about Wes?" I asked.

"Yeah, finally. He started following me home from school and when I showed Mom the note he left in my locker one day, she called the police. I guess Mom finally figured he'd crossed a line."

"Did you have to testify at his trial?"

"Yes, and it was horrible. The only good thing was that the judge cleared the courtroom and only the lawyers and the jury were there. Wes scared me, the way he looked at me when I answered the questions the lawyers asked. His lawyer tried to say that I was the one chasing Wes. That I had a crush on him. That was so creepy."

"Did the jury believed you?"

"Yes, and I thought that was the end of it. Until he showed up for band practice when I was with Bobby. I almost threw up. I just quit coming to the band's gigs and stayed away from Wes."

"Didn't Bobby wonder why?"

"Yes. I didn't want Bobby to know about the trial. When Bobby thought that I wasn't interested in him anymore, I finally had to tell him about Wes and how he stalked me. Bobby was furious and I think he said something to Wes, because he never talked to me or anything after that first time. So, I started going with the band again. I think Bobby and I are even closer than before."

"I'm sure the detectives have asked you this, Sally. Where were you on Thursday night when Wes was killed?"

Sally looked down and said, "We just went home. I mean, he dropped me off at my place then he went home. I was tired and we didn't want to stop and eat with the others and stay out half the night. We both had to work on Friday—well, I thought I had to work. I didn't know the building would be closed."

"Did your mother hear you come in? Did she know what time that was?"

"Mom wasn't there. She went to Minnetonka to visit her sister. My aunt hasn't been well lately. She has cancer and the chemo is pretty hard on her. Mom went to take care of her for a few days."

I walked with Sally back to the Home Arts Building and found Mark having a rush of business. We all pitched in and after about a half hour business slowed down and I headed for my car to pick up Megan. When I passed the mid-sized tent, I glanced in, half expecting to see Natalie sitting there as she was last night. Instead, I watched as Clara from Ray's band walked toward the entrance.

"Hi, Clara." I greeted her.

"Hi." She walked past me. I figured she didn't remember me.

"Clara," I called to her. "Do you have a minute?"

"Me? What for?"

"I'm Jennifer. I met you at the keg tapping on Thursday night."

Oh, ya'. You're the one who found Wes. What can I do for you?" She looked around as if to find a way to get away from me.

"You know that the police think my friend, Sister Bernadine killed Wes. Can I ask you a couple questions?"

"What kind of questions? I really don't know anything and I've talked to the police several times."

"No, not about Wes. I was at the closing last night in the big tent. How long have you known Trudy?" I asked.

"Trudy? Oh, gee, we've been friends since high school. She's a little older than me, so we didn't hang around until high school," Clara answered

"Do you know why she has such an attitude

about the Fest Meister?"

Clara snorted. "You bet. She and Frank were an item in high school. They were the prom king and queen. He was the star center of the hockey team and she was the head cheerleader. It was a storybook romance, without the happy ending."

"What happened?"

"College happened. Frank went to college on a hockey scholarship at the University of Minnesota. He had dreams of playing in the NHL. Trudy went to Hermann Community College and got her Associates Degree in Office Systems. Then Frank met Ida. I don't know how they got together but he fell in love with Ida and that's all she wrote. Hook, line and sinker, he fell. They got married, she got pregnant, and Frank had to quit school to support them. Ida was from the Twin Cities but they moved here when he dropped out of college.

"The problem was that Frank never broke up with Trudy. He just quit writing and calling and then he shows up here with a pregnant wife. Trudy was not only heartbroken. She was shocked and embarrassed.

"That had to be horrible for her."

"It was. She married Ray about six months later. Right after Frank and Ida's baby was born. They've had a good life and I believe she really loves Ray. Now. But it was hard for her. At the time, she thought everyone in town was laughing at her behind her back. No one was laughing at her."

"Maybe not." I said, "But pity can be worse."

"You betcha. So now you can see why she don't particularly like old Frank, our show off Fest Meister."

"What about Frank and Ida. Are they still married?"

"Ida died a few years ago. Cancer. Frank was still crazy about her all these years. Anything she wanted, he gave her. Worked his butt off, he did. And she was plenty demanding. I think today they'd call her 'high maintenance.'"

Too Dead to Dance

15

You've been baking," I said, giving her a hug. "You're just in time to test-taste my espresso brownies. Don always dunks his pastry in his coffee so I thought I'd invent these for him."

She plopped a pan of brownies on the counter. I sat down on a white padded bar stool. Megan's bar stools were so comfortable we could sit here for hours. Besides being padded, they had wooden arms and swiveled.

Megan pored us each a big cup of java, adding a dollop of coffee liqueur for good measure to each cup. Then she cut into the brownies and put a large square in front of me. Picking it up with my fingers, I took a big bite. Yummy rich chocolate and a hint of coffee.

Munching on a delicious brownie I said, "So, things are back on with Don?" Megan frowned at me. "What do you mean? It was never off."

"Well, you were with that other guy on Thursday night. I just thought . . ."

"Jennifer, you think too much. Al was just for fun. Both of us were just looking for a diversion."

"Al? Did you say Al? Al Metzger?"

"Yeah. Do you know him? Oh, lord, you're blushing. Don't tell me you fell for his line?"

Sitting up straighter on the bar stool, I

straightened out my shirt and said, "Of course not. I just met him last night and we talked for a few minutes."

"Hah! Al doesn't talk, he flirts and gropes." Megan laughed and pointed her finger at me.

"Well, he didn't grope me! But he did flirt. Later I saw him driving through the fest grounds with one of the Polka Daze princesses."

"He's a real player," Megan said.

"He's more than a player. He's a suspect." I told Megan about Al and Wes not getting along. "Wait a minute. You were with Al on Thursday night. Guess that gets him off my suspect list."

Megan looked like she was about to say something, and then shook her head.

Changing the subject, I asked, "How did you make these wonderful brownies? I didn't even know you baked."

"I cheated, of course. I started with, 'Open one package of brownie mix...' Then I added some espresso and other goodies. I even put some coffee liqueur in the frosting. Do you like it?"

"It's wonderful! You need to write down the recipe so I can make them."

Halfway through my second brownie, Megan's phone chirped. She looked at the screen, giggled, and then started tapping the keys.

I waited a few minutes, thinking she was being a little rude letting me sit there staring at her while messages went flying back and forth. Finally, she noticed I was getting impatient and ended the session.

I assumed it was Don who took her full attention. "Why didn't he just call if he wanted to talk to you?"

"He's on a plane, on his way to Las Vegas." "You're kidding! He's texting while flying a plane?"

Megan snickered while pouring another cup of coffee for me along with another dollop of coffee liqueur.

"No, he bummed a ride to Las Vegas. He's meeting some friends from college for a guy thing. He's just waiting for take-off. And he wasn't texting he was sexting."

"What the heck is that?"

"Sexy talk."

"You mean you were having phone sex while I was sitting right here? That's so disgusting."

Sometime I wish I couldn't read upside down. I glanced at Megan's phone and saw, "I can't wait to kiss your pretty . . ." I jerked my head back and gasped.

The corners of Megan's eyes crinkled as she grinned at me, showing no remorse what so ever. "Quit being such a prude. You sound like Bernie."

Realizing she was right, I laughed with her. "Just promise me you won't send him any naked pictures."

"I may be silly but I'm not stupid. Those things can follow you around the rest of your life."

After we pigged out, I told her about Sally and Bobby. They were each other's alibi but both had said they were alone after Bobby dropped off Sally. "Something was wrong though. Sally wouldn't look at me while she told me about Bobby dropping her off. I can't believe that sweet Sally could do something as horrible as murdering someone."

When I finished telling her all I had learned since yesterday, she poured us each a glass of Madeira wine. She said it was the perfect dessert wine. "How did Wes know Sally's father?"

"I don't have a clue. I suppose he was a guard or patron at the bank." We both looked at her computer at the same time.

When we Googled "bank robbery + Hermann, MN," there were only two hits. One was in 1928 and the other four years ago.

"I remember that," Megan said. "It was a big deal around here. Do you remember it?"

"Vaguely. This happened about the time I was busy planning Beth's wedding. I'm glad I only had one daughter. If Nick ever gets married, all I have to do is show up."

"You keep thinking that, Sweetie." Megan said, patting me on the back. She had three kids, two boys and a girl. Carrie was the only one still single.

As we perused down the newspaper article we came to his name. "David Baumgartner, well known to the police due to numerous arrests for misdemeanors from DWI to bad checks, was shot and killed by the bank guard, Roger Olmsted. The two other robbers got away in a black sedan."

"Oh, Lord, Sally's father was the bank robber," I said. "That must have been difficult for her family. No wonder Wes had been able to weasel his way into their trust."

"And no wonder Sally's mother clung to him and refused to believe Sally might be in danger," Megan added.

"I think Wes may have been one of the bank robbers."

"Whoa, that's jumping to a big conclusion, Sweetie." "I know, but I have a feeling this is all related somehow. I'm going over to talk to Marty."

"Are you nuts? Edwin will never let you in the house. What are you going to say, 'Did your husband rob a bank before he got sent up for stalking little girls?' I'm coming with you. This I have to see."

"Give me some credit. I know how to be tactful, unlike some people I know. If you insist on going with me, watch what you say. I don't want to spook her. By the way, Edwin goes to twelve o'clock Mass every Sunday."

"You're kidding."

'Nope, he tries to keep up his image as a pious man. I doubt if anyone but Edwin believes that."

We left Megan's house and walked toward my car. I noticed the bags from the Christmas Shop, again. "Meg, I need to run these over to my place. I keep forgetting them. I'll be right back."

I grabbed the bags and pulled them out of the

car. A piece of paper fluttered to the ground. I bent over, picking it up from the grass, not wanting to litter Megan's front yard. It looked like a receipt but I remembered putting that in my purse after I signed the charge slip. Unfolding the paper, I read in thick black lettering, "STOP SNOOPING!!!"

I dropped the bags. Luckily, I was standing on the grass not the driveway and the bags thumped but I didn't hear any glass breaking. Megan rushed to my side of the car.

"What's wrong?" She asked, grabbing the note from my hand. Megan read the note then looked at me. "Who wrote this? Where did it come from?"

"I don't know who wrote it. It was in one of these bags." I picked up my parcels and walked across the street.

Megan trailed behind me. "Where are you going? What are you going to do about it?"

Stopping in the middle of the street, I turned and answered. "I'm going to put these bags in my house. Then I'm going over to talk to Marty. Are you coming with me?"

"Of course, I'm with you all the way. Shouldn't you call Decker and tell him about it?"

"No. He'll just tell me to keep my nose out of it before I get hurt."

"Maybe he's right. This is getting 'way too scary."

"I don't care. I'm angry." Waving the paper in her face, I replied between clenched teeth, "How dare someone break into my car and leave a note like this for me. Who does this person think he is?"

Megan took the bags from me and said, "I'll put these in your house, get the car and we'll go to Marty's.

Too Dead to Dance

Diane Morlan

16

We drove the familiar route to Winfield Heights, a newer subdivision on the east side of Hermann. When we pulled into the driveway of the house on Willow Street where I had lived for the past four years, a pain ripped through my chest and I had to blink fast to hold the tears back. I spied the red and white "For Sale" sign stuck on a post in the front yard and my lips quivered.

"I thought Edwin had listed the house with you," I said to Megan.

"Nope. He went with Hermann Realty. You know, now that I think about it, I'm pretty sure Marty's brother works there."

"Well, that's just great. I'm not using my part of the profits to pay for the realtor. He'll have to fight me for it."

We climbed the three steps to the little front porch and rang the bell.

I remembered when we had moved here, Edwin was unhappy with his transfer. He felt as if he'd been demoted, even though he was now head of the accounting department with a substantial pay raise. He'd lived all his life in Chicago suburbs and believed we were now living among hicks, in a small town with no "culture." Not that he ever attended anything cultural in Chicago, unless you count an occasional Bears game when someone gave him tickets.

While he grumped and groaned about everything for

the first year, I spent that time turning our new two-story home into a "House Beautiful." I had wanted us to buy a classic old Colonial Revival right in the heart of Hermann but Edwin wanted to live in a "classier" part of town. Because I believed that he made the forty mile commute so I could live near my friends, I gave in. I usually gave in to Edwin. I didn't seem to have any trouble standing up to friends and strangers but for some reason Edwin intimidated me.

I finally gave in to his brow beating for this two-story home with a three-car garage stuck right in front as if the cars, not people were most important. Edwin had a patio built in the back yard and declined to sit on the tiny front porch. He said he refused to look like Farmer Brown, sitting in a rocker, drinking moonshine. Instead, he sat on his patio drinking inexpensive Merlot, which he hated but was all the rage at the time.

I rang the front door bell again and waited for Marty to answer. I was sure she hadn't accompanied Edwin to church. He was trying to keep the fact that Marty was living here low key. I thought if his reputation was so dear to him perhaps he shouldn't behave like a louse.

When Marty opened the door, wearing a jewel colored wrap and looking good, even with her hair all tousled, I regretted not thinking of how we wanted to approach Marty about the questions I needed answered.

"Uh, hi," I said, trying to sound upbeat. Too bad, it sounded squeaky. "Could we talk to you for a few minutes?"

Marty stood up straighter, took a deep breath, and said, "Look, Jennifer, Edwin's not here. Can't you just wait for a few days until I'm out of here before you come back? I'll be gone soon."

"Marty, I don't know what you're talking about. Why are you leaving?"

"Oh, crap. Come on in." Marty opened the door wider and turned. She walked down the hall to the kitchen where I had spent so much time in the past four years.

I peeked into the rooms as we passed them. The dining room looked the same as always, but the living room was different. She had rearranged the furniture. I had to admit, it looked better with the sofa on the outside wall and the armchairs cozying up to the fireplace. I had never been able to make that room look comfortable and Marty accomplished it by just moving the furniture around. I was impressed.

I sat down at my '50's style red and white kitchen table. Marty sniffled. "Edwin and I had a terrible fight. He accused me of taking advantage of him. I only put a few things on his charge card and if he didn't want me to use it, he shouldn't have left it on the counter. Then he accused me of sneaking around behind his back."

"I'm sorry Marty. I don't want Edwin back. I'm here because my best friend has been accused of killing your ex-husband. Is there anything you know that could help us clear her?"

"Why should I care about your friends? Wes was a bully. Maybe she did us all a favor. Where the hell am I going to live? I gave up my apartment to move here. Damn. I should've known better. Men are such nincompoops."

I did my best to keep a straight face as I returned the conversation to the reason we had come here. "What were you and Wes arguing about the night he was killed? I heard you talked to him at Polka Fest."

"So, it was you who told Edwin that I didn't come right home from Jazzercise. He'd just gotten the Visa statement and it put him over the top. Now I have to find a job and a place to live. Thanks a lot."

"Was Wes involved in the bank robbery where David Baumgartner was killed?" As long as she hadn't thrown us out, I figured I might as well ask.

She heaved a big sighed and then her shoulders relaxed. "I don't know. I always thought Wes had been in on that bank robbery. He wouldn't admit it and I sure didn't see any of the money. He was acting real crazy, though. He'd peek out the front window while standing behind the curtain. He'd jump a foot if the phone rang and wouldn't let me answer until he checked the caller ID. He got locked up about two months later. I thought that it was because of the stalking that made him so crazy."

I was about to ask another question when she started talking again.

"When he was sent to St. Cloud Penitentiary he told me to wait for him and all of our problems would be over when he got out. He kept hinting that when he was paroled we would've a great life together. That's when I started to connect him to the bank robbery. That's what I was talking to him about Thursday night. If he had some money, I deserved my share for putting up with him. But, he was still mad because I didn't wait and divorced him while he was in prison. What a jerk."

I decided not to tell her she had a habit of falling for jerks. Before I could think of anything else to ask her, she stood up and told us goodbye. We followed her to the door and before I could thank her, she shut the door. At least she didn't slam it.

"Wow," said Megan. "That was sure gutsy. Sweetie, I didn't know you had it in you. Way to go."

I walked over to the attached garage and peeked through the window. "What are you doing? Let's get out of here before she decides to call the cops."

"She's not going to call anyone. She drives a navy blue Blazer. She could be the one who ran me off the road last night."

We walked back to my Civic. I leaned down to open the door and pain streaked up the back of my neck. I hadn't needed any painkiller since before Mass this morning. I cried out and Megan grabbed my arm.

She helped me into the passenger seat of my car.

Megan slid behind the wheel and backed out of the driveway. "We're going to the hospital."

"Don't be silly, it'll go away. I just need some ibuprofen."

"You need more than that. For starters, you need an x-ray."

Against my protests, Megan drove to Hermann Hospital. While we waited on stiff green chairs, Megan suggested that we make a list of suspicious people.

"A suspect list? What a great idea!" I fished around in my purse and came up with my new little notebook.

Megan looked at the notebook and I saw the sides of her mouth turn up. "Leave me alone," I said.

"A regular little Nancy Drew, aren't you?"

"Shut up." At least she referred to me as a young detective and not Jessica Fletcher.

We started the list off with the band members. "I don't know if anyone besides Bobby had a gripe with Wes, but they all knew him. And the Fest Meister said that the band is up to something."

"What does that mean?" asked Megan.

"I don't know but I plan to find out. It was something between Ray, Clara, and Vic. I think Wes and Bobby were excluded."

"Who else?" asked Megan.

"I don't know. The Fest Meister said that Wes was a stinker and lots of people had it in for him. I think we need to find out who some of those people are."

Of course, we happily added Marty.

"Who else? We can't add Al. You were with him. How about Bobby? Maybe Bobby and Sally were together but they both could've... What am I saying? Sally is too sweet to hurt anyone."

Megan took a deep breath and said, "About Al..." "Go in there and a nurse will help you," the Receptionist said, interrupting our conversation. In this small hospital, there were only three examination areas. The curtains were open on two of them. My feet dangled as I sat on the gurney assigned to me. My head pounded while electric shocks shot up and down my neck. Soon

Too Dead to Dance

Lisa Vetter came in, closed the curtains around Megan and me, and stuck a thermometer in my ear.

"Are you the one who sent the cops after my husband this morning?" she asked, clicking the thermometer, and then reading the results a few seconds later.

"I'm so sorry; Lisa, but I had no choice. The police wanted to know what happened last night and Randy was Bernie's alibi."

"No he wasn't. The police think Randy helped her kill that guy."

"Did they say that?" I asked.

"No, but I could tell that's what they were thinking. I don't like Randy being involved in something as nasty as murder."

"I don't like my friend, Bernie, being a suspect either. I thought Randy would help the police stop accusing her and look for the real killer."

"Well, it didn't work out that way, did it? You can bet all the neighbors were checking out the police car in the driveway. Is this what he gets for being nice to a nun? I guess no good deed goes unpunished."

Megan set down the magazine she had just moved from the chair when she sat down. "How can they think Randy is involved? He was with you when it happened. He fixed her car on Friday morning, didn't he?"

"No. He went over on Thursday night and aired-up the two flat tires, then called Bernie. She asked him to pick her up and bring her over to the Fest Grounds. She didn't want to leave her car there all night."

"Okay," I said. "So, Randy followed her home and can vouch for her whereabouts, right?"

"Wrong." Lisa sighed then shook her head. "Randy wanted to follow her home. She told him that she needed to check out something and that Randy should go ahead and go home. He offered to go with her but she refused. She said it was something she had to take care of herself."

"What time was this, do you know?" I asked.

"I don't know. No, wait. Jim said that when he pulled out to leave he got caught up in the traffic from people leaving the parking lot. So, it must have been right after the closing ceremony at the big tent. That's when most people leave, isn't it?"

"Why on earth would Bernie be going to the Fest Grounds when everyone else was leaving?" I asked.

No one answered.

I apologized again and Lisa said it was okay but I could tell she was still in a snit with me for getting her husband involved.

Too Dead to Dance

17

Almost two hours later, we walked out of the hospital. Megan drove because I couldn't move my neck without twisting my whole torso. The foam neck brace helped the pain and Lisa promised the medications the doctor had prescribed would do the trick. In my hand, I held a prescription for thirty tablets of Tylenol with codeine. We stopped to get the prescription filled at Richter's Drug Store.

While waiting for the pharmacist to fill my prescription, we sat down on the cold plastic chairs. Megan started digging in her enormous black purse, even bigger than mine. She leered wickedly at me and pulled out a sweating bottle of blue wine cooler.

"Where did you get that? Put it away before we get in trouble."

She cracked the twist cap and took a long swig then handed the bottle to me. "I swiped it from Edwin's fridge. He'll never miss it. I was going to drink it at the ER but I thought someone might try to detox me or send me to A.A. Go ahead, take a swig."

"We can't drink here," I protested.

"Why not? I don't see a sign with a martini glass and a red line through it."

"We could get arrested, Megan. Put it away."

"Oh, bull. There's no law against drinking at the drug store."

Too Dead to Dance

Laughing, I took a swig. It felt so naughty, but fun. No wonder I loved Meg so much. She always got me to do inane things I would never have thought of myself.

Medications in hand, minus the two pills I had swilled down with the last of the wine cooler, we pulled out of the parking lot towards the Fest Grounds. We didn't get far. Three sawhorses blocked the road and we could hear the sirens in the distance announcing the beginning of the parade.

When we realized this side of town would be at a standstill until after the parade, Megan turned the car around and pulled back into the parking space we had just vacated.

Leaving the car parked at Richter's Drug Store, we pulled a couple folding canvas chairs out of the trunk, a staple in most cars in Minnesota in the summer. We walked around the corner and found two young men to help us put up our chairs before they sat back down on the curb.

We settled in right before we had to stand for the color guard and the beginning of the parade. After they went past, I gratefully sat down feeling light-headed and woozy from the pills and the wine.

Like most small town parades, it started with all the fire trucks in the area driving along with sirens blaring, which made my head hurt all over again. Next came several convertibles carrying the elite of Hermann—the mayor, and other city dignitaries.

I waved at them and called out the names written on signs pasted to the side of the cars. Megan tried to shush me, saying, "You probably shouldn't have mixed the meds with wine cooler. It's making you goofy."

"Like it was my idea. Leave me alone, I'm just having fun. You sound like Edwin."

Megan laughed and shook her head. "You go, girl. Have fun."

Several businesses followed in their vehicles, including the Metzger's Meat Market red panel truck with a fat little butcher holding a string of sausages painted on the side. "There's your sweetie, Al," I told Megan and everyone else within earshot, "Did you know he almost ran me down at the Fest Grounds Friday morning?"

Megan was trying to shut me up, or at least quiet me down when I was smacked in the side of the head with a Dum-Dum Sucker. "Ouch!" I hollered, picking up the lollipop. "Grape! My favorite." I ripped the wrapper off and stuck it in my mouth.

Most of the entries in the parade, including Frank and Al Metzger, had several kids walking along side of their vehicle or float, throwing candy to the delight of the plastic bag bearing children who ran to grab their share. Al Metzger, looking as cute as he did last night when he was flirting with me, waved and called out to people by name, laughing.

Megan and I looked at each other and shrugged our shoulders. I still didn't approve of her cheating on Don but she was my friend, no matter what. Al's brother, Frank sat shotgun waving at the folks on the other side of the street. Behind him was Ben's Furniture Barn delivery truck, followed by Pizza Palace's drivers in cars with the lighted triangular logo stuck to the top.

The Hermann Carnegie Library's Book Cart Precision Drill Team has always been my favorite entry in all our town parades. I clapped my hands as I watched them march down the street toward us. The book carts were decorated with swaying silver tinsel and signs announcing the library's web site—www.hermannlib.org.

The eight ladies pushing the carts were the two reference librarians, the three library assistants, and three of the women who ran the "Friends of the Library" organization that helped the library with much needed funds for new books. The library had tried to find a man for the last open librarian position, but none applied.

The ladies were dressed in colorful flowered skirts and big floppy straw hats decorated with flowers that matched their skirts. Their matching white t-shirts sported the slogan, *Do You Know Where Your Library Books Are?*

They marched down the street in strict order, occasionally sashaying in and out making a figure eight. Then they moved to the curb, still pushing the fancy book carts and shushed the crowd in exaggerated form. We all laughed and applauded our library's drill team.

Following the librarians, the Hermann High School band marched up the street, the students sweating in their heavy uniforms in the mid-summer sunshine. Hot and thirsty myself, I wished someone would squirt cold water into my mouth the way the volunteer mothers did for the strutting kids.

The two young men on the curb laughed and drank Cokes from a cooler at their feet. Megan finally sweet-talked them into sharing their stash, promising them a pound of fresh roasted coffee after the parade. Good thing I had fifty pounds in the back seat of my car.

After about an hour, the last entry in the parade, KHER-FM radio station's employees handed out freeze pops from coolers in the back of their van. Three police officers on motorcycles brought up the rear. People grabbed their chairs and headed for their cars. We took our time, enjoying the break for as long as possible, knowing it would be a while before we would be able to get to the Fest Grounds through the traffic.

While we waited for the crowd to thin out, I asked Megan if she thought Sally and Bobby could be involved in Wes' murder.

"I suppose anything is possible, Jennifer. This whole thing is crazy. I don't want to believe anyone I know could've killed another human being."

I had to find out what kind of car Bobby drove. Sally had recently bought an older Dodge minivan, which was about the same size as the vehicle that ran me off the road but just didn't seem right. Also, it was more of a silver blue, way too light in color. Marty's SUV still best fit my image of that vehicle.

Megan drove toward her home. "Don will be landing in Minneapolis in about an hour and I don't want to miss his call. Are you okay to drive?"

"I'll be fine. Do you want to do something later, after I'm done at the Fest Grounds?"

"I don't know. I may go up and stay with him tonight. So, call my cell if you need to get a hold of me."

After she went into the house, I maneuvered into the driver's seat and slowly made my way to the Fest Grounds. No multi-tasking for me until this neck brace was off.

A half hour later, I walked into the Home Arts building bringing with me the much-needed coffee. "Where have you been?" Sally demanded. "I've been calling your cell for an hour. Oh my God! What happened to your neck? Are you okay?"

"I'm so sorry, Sally. I keep leaving you here to do all the work. I had a little accident last night but I'm okay. The brace keeps the pressure off my spine and helps with the pain," I explained in a rush. "Megan and I got stuck at the parade. It was pretty noisy; guess I couldn't hear my phone ringing. What's up?" I plopped down the coffee I had brought in from the car, minus the two pounds we gave to the guys at the parade.

"Detective Jacobs is looking for you. Something's happened. He just left. He said he went to your townhouse and we both tried to call you. You'd better call him right away."

"What's happened?" I asked while burrowing in my purse for my cell phone, a feeling of dread washing over me. "Oh, God. Do you think they arrested Bernie?"

"I don't know. I hope not. Call him and find out." "On second thought, I doubt Lieutenant Jacobs would drive all the way out here to tell me that."

Checking my phone, I found Jacob's missed call number and hit the "talk" button.

After a short conversation that told me nothing, I hung up. "He wants me down at the station. He said to bring Megan. She's my alibi. I don't know why I need an

Too Dead to Dance

alibi but I'd better pick up Megan and get down there."

I turned to Sally, "I'm sorry to leave you here again. Did Mark ever show up?"

"He's here. He went to get something for us to eat," She heaved a sigh. "We'll be fine here, just go. If you aren't back, we'll close up at six o'clock. We can all come in tomorrow morning to break down the booth and clean-up."

I thanked Sally, thinking I needed to give her a raise. And a bonus. "Sally, what kind of car does Bobby drive?"

"A dark blue Camaro. Why?"

"No reason, I thought I saw him at the parade. Must have been someone else."

I looked over to Trudy's booth. She wiggled her fingers my way and I knew she had taken in everything that had been said. I decided to ask her about the band.

Stepping over to her booth, I asked, "Trudy, I heard that Ray and Clara and Vic are up to something. Do you know what that is?"

"What are you talking about? Up to what?"

"I don't know. Someone saw the three of them whispering together several times."

"Well, of course they talk. They play together and there are all sorts of things they need to go over."

"No, I don't think that's what it was. It was just Ray and Clara and Vic, not Bobby or Wes."

Trudy laughed. "Oh, that. They were planning my surprise birthday party."

"How can it be a surprise if you know about it?"

"They do it every year and every year I act surprised. Usually they have a Saturday night gig in one of the taverns around here. They invite all of our friends, I show up, and act surprised. We have a great time. Do you want to be put on the guest list this year? It's next month."

"I'd love to. Thanks."

"Jennifer, who told you that about the band?"

"Well, I really shouldn't say, Trudy.

"Frank. It was Frank wasn't it? He's such a blabbermouth. He never could keep his big mouth shut."

Too Dead to Dance

18

I called Megan while driving to her house. Lucky for me, she'd just hung up from talking to Don so I got right through to her.

"I was just going to leave for Minneapolis, Jennifer." "Meg, I really need you to go with me. Detective Jacobs told Sally he wanted to see both of us. I think they arrested Bernie."

"Did Sally tell you that?"

"No, but why else would he want to see us?"

"A better question is why would he want to see us if he's arrested Bernie? Okay, I'll call Don. I'll wait on the porch for you."

When we pulled into the parking lot at the county courthouse, I told Megan, "I called Jacobs and he said to come to the side door and ring the buzzer."

We found the door and next to it was a big red button. I pushed the button and could hear an obnoxious bell ringing inside the building.

A uniformed deputy came to the door and when I explained that Lieutenant Jacobs was expecting us, he escorted us back to a large room filled with about a dozen desks. I looked around for Detective Decker but only three people were in the room-- a young woman and a redheaded guy, both in uniform at desks near the door.

Behind a desk in the corner sat Jacobs in a wrinkled blue suit. Someone needed to buy this man an iron. He stood up as we approached, grabbed a file off his desk and ushered us to an interview room. Like those seen on television, it was a small grey room with a scratched table and a few stiff metal chairs. We sat.

Jacobs positioned a manila folder in front of him and squared the corners precisely. "Were you over at your husband's house today, Jennifer?"

"It's still my house, too." I replied, sitting up straighter, my hands clenching into fists. "Edwin had better not try to keep me from there. I still have a half interest in the house."

"Is that what happened? Did Marty Fischer tell you to go away?"

"No. Actually, she was reasonably civil, considering we barged in on her. I did see her SUV in the garage. I think she's the person who ran me off the road. She had an argument with Wes at the Fest grounds. I think Wes was in on that bank robbery four years ago and Marty wanted some money from him.

Jacobs waited while I wound down, then looked at me and said, "Someone killed Marty Fischer."

I sat there with my mouth gapping open. I think my heart stopped beating for a second. "What happened? Who killed her? Did someone do this in my house? Oh, my God." I glanced at Megan. Her mouth hung open, too.

I snapped my mouth shut when I understood Jacobs suspected us, but Megan jumped right in. "Wait a minute; we didn't do anything to Marty. She was alive when we left the house. We talked to her in the kitchen, then left."

Jacobs nodded. "I know. The neighbor saw you leave. She also saw Sister Bernadine's car pull up shortly after you left. Did you tell Sister Bernadine about your conversation with Marty?"

"Oh, Mrs. Johnson, the neighborhood snoop.

What does Bernie have to do with this?" I felt my head spinning as if in some sort of vortex. Scenes whirled in my head until something connected.

"Oh, my God," Megan said. "Bernie was the last person to see her alive, wasn't she?"

Jacobs looked at me, than Megan. He folded his hands over the folder and said, "Okay, now you tell me where Sister Bernadine is and don't jack me around. Okay?"

I sat there, tears running down my cheeks. "I haven't seen her since church this morning."

"You went to Mass with her this morning?" Jacobs asked.

I swiped away my tears with the back of my hand. "No. I came late, but I talked to her before I left."

"Do you have any idea where she might be now, Jennifer?"

"I don't know why you keep thinking Bernie could do something like this. She wouldn't hurt anyone—ever. What happened to Marty? How was she killed and who found her? And what the heck was Bernie doing there?" "Jennifer, I think you forget who is doing the questioning here. I'm the police, remember? Now where is Sister Bernadine?"

"I don't know. I'm her friend, not her keeper." My head began to clear after the shock of hearing about another murder in our little town. "If, in fact she was there, someone else must have come by later and killed her. Who called it in?"

"There you go again, asking the questions." Jacobs said, practically biting his tongue to keep from laughing.

"I don't see any humor here, Lieutenant Jacobs." I sat up straighter and pushed out my chest, trying to look insulted. "Someone has been killed and you need to find the person who did it."

"Yes, Jennifer, and if I knew where Sister Bernadine was, I could ask her if she saw anything unusual while she was there. Or when she was leaving."

"Wait a minute. Aren't you looking at other suspects? What about the other members of the band? They were probably closest to him."

"They all have alibis. And there you go again."

"No. No they don't. Did you talk to Bobby's parents? Was he home?"

"Bobby doesn't live with his parents. He and his brother share an apartment, but he wasn't home Thursday night; his brother said he was with his girlfriend."

"No, he wasn't. Sally told me he dropped her off and then went home."

"Maybe Sally didn't want you to know he was with her. I told you, Jennifer. People lie all the time. But we'll check it out."

Jacobs finally decided he'd learned all we knew, but we hadn't found out much about Marty's death from him. We knew that she'd been killed in the kitchen. I'm almost ashamed to admit my first thought was that now we'd never get the house sold.

Jacobs walked us to the door and told us to be available if he needed to talk to us again. "And, ladies, make sure you call me or Detective Decker if you see Sister Bernadine. This is important, so don't go trying to hide her or anything."

We assured him that we would be good citizens and have Bernie call him if we saw her. I didn't mention that I would find out everything I could from her before I had her contact the Sheriff's Office.

We walked out the door of the station and this time I almost knocked Detective Decker down the stairs.

"Ohmygod!" I grabbed his left arm to help him get his balance. "Are you okay?"

He swept me up in his right arm and pulled me close. "I'm fine, Jennifer. Good Lord, what happened to your neck? Is that from your accident last night?"

I kind of liked having his arm around me. "Yes, but I'm fine. Really"

"I see Jacobs didn't arrest either of you."

I pushed him away, even though I wanted to melt into his chest and forget about everything else. I straightened out my sweater while I caught my breath and noticed a tiny little spot of wine cooler I had spilled on myself. "What's going on? Who killed, Marty?"

"Ah, Jennifer, do you really think I'm going to tell you anything?" He wrapped his arm around me again and gave me a squeeze then let me go. Just before he turned and disappeared through the station door, he winked at me.

"Oh, girl," Megan cooed, "You've got it bad. And he is a gorgeous hunk of man, even though he's petite."

"He's not petite. Girls are petite. He's, well, compact. And he is a hunk, but I'm not going to start dating him until he admits that Bernie is innocent."

"Dating? Do people still date? Jennifer, what if he's right about Bernie? She has a fierce temper."

"Megan! How can you even think such a thing? I know she can get ticked off and yell a lot but she's never gotten physical with anyone. At least not since she grew up. Shame on you for even thinking such a thought."

"Okay, then shame on me. Then you tell me where she was on Thursday night? What the heck was she doing at the Fest Grounds when everyone else was leaving? The only people left were the hard drinkers and some of the bands." Megan was so worked up she shook her finger at me. "I know she's not a hard drinker, so that leaves—"

"Meg, I know it looks bad—"

"Wait!" She held up her hand. "She was up to something. I know. She wouldn't hurt a fly, but she was up to something and we need to find out what that was. If we could find her we could ask and get to the bottom of this."

"Well, let's go look for her. We can drive by her house and see if her car is there. Then—"

"Wait a minute, Jennifer! I'm sure the police have been to her house and the church. Where else might she go?"

I grabbed my phone and found Bernie's sister's number in my contact list. Punching the button, I listened to it ring four times then it went to voice mail.

"Nope, not there. Where else would she hide out?" "Maybe she's not hiding. Maybe she doesn't know what happened and she's just going about her business," Megan said.

We drove around town for a while, checking out Chick's Drive-in and Riverview Movie Theater. We cruised around town for almost an hour. Finally, Megan said, "I give up. Take me home. If we can't find her the cops never will."

I dropped off Megan, suspecting she wanted to do some sexting with Don since she wouldn't be seeing him between flights this week. Before she got out of the car, she turned to me and put her hand on my arm.

"Jennifer, I have a confession to make."

"Oh, not more hanky-panky, Megan. I'm not sure I want to hear about it.

"No, no. Not anything like that. In fact, just the opposite. I didn't sleep with Al. We just messed around for a while, and then I sent him home."

"Why on earth did you tell me you slept with him?" "I didn't. You just jumped to that conclusion. It ticked me off so I decided to just let you think whatever you wanted."

"Oh, Megan, I'm so sorry! I should've known better."

"Yes, you should have. More important, what other conclusions have you jumped to? Think about the people you've talked to. Is there anything you may have missed by not looking at details and just assuming something?"

"I don't know. I'll think about it. You know, that puts Al back on the suspect list."

Megan shivered. "I hope it wasn't him. I'd hate to think I kissed a killer."

I headed for Dottie's Diner to grab a bite to eat. Dottie's is a truck stop on the corner where Maron County Road 9 and the state highway cross at the bottom of a hill, across the river right outside the city limits. Like the members of the Windig Sangers, people flocked there after the bars closed because it was the only place open that late.

I pulled into a parking space near the front door under the blinking lights announcing "Good Eats." Looking around, I spotted a blue Aveo between two SUV's and knew I had stumbled on the one place we hadn't thought to look for Bernie.

I walked through the front part of the building where the convenience store and checkout counter were located. Past the rest rooms that also housed showers for the truckers and on to the brightly lit diner in the back part of the building. Dottie's had been our favorite hangout when we were in high school. We often met here to discuss our latest conquests and disasters. With all the craziness going on in Hermann, Dottie's felt like a sane, safe place to be. At least it felt that way to me as I slipped into the back booth across from Bernie.

"Fancy meeting you here," I said.

Waving her hand around in a circle over her head, Bernie said, "We haven't been here together in a long time."

The waitress arrived and I ordered a cheeseburger, fries, and a Coke. After she walked away, I realized I hadn't even looked at the menu. I just ordered what I had always ordered here, even though I hadn't been here since I was fifteen.

"You heard about Marty?" I asked and blew into the cup in front of her. "I can't believe it. I keep wondering if the person who killed her was in the house when I was there. That's such a scary thought, but she seemed okay, not frightened or anything, so I think she was alone," she said wiping the condensation off her glasses with her index finger. "I'm trying to remember what cars were parked on the street. I'm in trouble, aren't I?" She sat there eerily calm. Not at all the in-your-face woman I had grown to love.

"I think so, Bernie. Jacobs and Decker want to see you so they probably have a lot of questions."

"And I don't have the answers, Jennifer. I saw her and talked to her, and then I left. She was very angry with me but she was alive."

"Why did you go to her house, for Pete's sake?" I demanded.

"I thought she'd killed Wes. I told her I would go with her to the police and stay with her through the whole process. She cussed me out and told me to mind my own business. Jennifer, I thought she had the money from the bank robbery and wouldn't give it to Wes and he got aggressive and she was defending herself."

"I know you were just trying to help but, Bernie that was dangerous. If she'd killed Wes she could've attacked you."

"I suppose so. I didn't think of that. She called me a fool, Jennifer. I guess she was right. What do I know about these things? I should mind my own business. If I had arrived later, I would've seen who did this to her. Or, if I had stayed longer, maybe the person who killed her would've gone away. I feel so sad and guilty."

"You have nothing to feel guilty about. You didn't do anything. If you had stayed longer, you might have been hurt or killed, too. I'm starting to get ticked off at whoever did this. He's causing all of us a lot of problems. Somehow we'll find out what did happen to her and you can count on that."

"How are we going to do that?"

"I don't know yet but you need a good night's sleep and so do I. Why don't you call Jacobs and tell him you'll come in first thing tomorrow. You need to go home and get some rest. You don't want to talk to him now, you're too upset."

    I sat there feeling helpless while she called Lieutenant Jacobs and was surprised when he agreed. I guess he actually believed her explanation if he agreed to let her go home. We walked out to the parking lot and I wrapped my arms around her and told her to get some sleep. I would be at her house at eight o'clock tomorrow morning to go with her to the Sheriff's Department.

Too Dead to Dance

19

Turning onto Minnesota Street, I saw something on my front stoop. It looked like a large bundle. When I swung the Honda into the driveway, my headlights swept over the bundle and it began to move. It was a person. He stood up and walked toward my car.

I locked the doors and shifted into reverse, prepared to back out of the driveway and head to somewhere safe. As the figure came closer, I recognized Edwin. Opening the window, I yelled at him. "What's the matter with you, scaring me like that? Don't you know there's a killer running around loose?"

"Jennifer, I need your help. Marty is dead." He burst into tears.

Good Lord, after an excruciating day I thought would never end, Edwin expected me to comfort him. He looked so pitiful I actually felt sorry for him.

Shaking my head, I sighed, resigned to the fact the day might never end.

"Come in, Edwin."

I pulled into the garage, got out of the car and ushered Edwin into my kitchen, closing the squeaking garage door behind him.

I put on the coffeepot, selecting a hearty flavored decaf. I didn't need to stimulate him, just get him to calm down enough to go away. I had planned for us to sit in the kitchen but Edwin strolled into the living room, checking it out. I steered him toward my uncomfortable sofa, keeping the comfy chair for myself.

"Jennie, I don't know what I'm going to do. I loved her so much." Edwin put his head in his hands, completely oblivious to the fact that what he said might hurt me. As usual, it was all about him.

I couldn't bring myself to comfort him but I bit my tongue to keep from scolding him for calling me Jennie. "The police will find out who did this, Edwin." His head snapped up and he shouted, "They know who did it. You friend the nun killed my Marty. I hope she burns in hell!"

"Bernie did not kill Marty. Why would she do that?" "Because that nun murdered Wes and Marty knew it and she had to shut Marty up. And now my Marty is gone." He started sobbing again.

"Edwin, did Marty tell you Bernie killed Wes?"

"Of course not, but Marty was frightened about something and the deputies said Bernie was the last person at my house. When I got home from Mass, I walked in and found my Marty lying on the kitchen floor. There was so much blood. Now she's gone and I'll never be able to sell my house."

There was the Edwin I knew and used to love. His heart is broken and his thoughts are on the bottom line. At least I hadn't said it aloud when I thought of it.

"Did Marty tell you she was afraid of someone? How did she act when she found out Wes had been killed?"

"I don't know, Jennifer." He waved me away. He cocked his head, took a deep breath and began to answer my question. "She seemed sad at first. She cried and said now she'd never get her share. I thought she meant he had hid some assets from their marriage, but how could that be? He'd been in jail when they divorced years ago. I tried to comfort her but she pushed me away, grabbed her cell phone, and marched out of the room while punching the keys and mumbling about what she deserved."

I poured us some coffee and dug out a half-empty bag of Oreos that I found in my barren cupboard. Sitting across from him I asked, "So, Marty said you and she had a big fight and you told her to leave. What was that all about?"

"Oh, for God's sake, Jennifer, don't you start on me, too. The cops had a field day with that. Are you the one who told them about the fight?"

"No, Edwin. I never once considered you would kill Marty." To myself I added—you'd just be obnoxious, condescending, or belligerent.

"I got pissed because she took my Visa and charged almost $2000 on clothes and stuff. She must think I'm made of money."

"When did you and Marty have this fight?"

"I don't know, last night. I didn't mean it when I told her to get out. I was still pissed when I left for church but after Mass, I decided I could forgive her. I was planning to take her to lunch and letting her stay, if she promised not to touch my Visa again. Instead, I walk in and find her dead on my kitchen floor." He started a fresh round of tears.

Megan and I had left Marty shortly after twelve. Edwin would've arrived home by twelve-thirty, twelve forty-five at the latest. So, the killer came to the house after Bernie left and before Edwin came home. That considerably tightened up the time-line.

Someone no one saw or noticed came into the house after Bernie left. That part of town didn't have alleys, so the killer had to walk around the house to enter by the back door. The neighbors had remembered Bernie because she wore a habit. The person who came there after Bernie must have been in some way invisible to the people in the neighborhood. Somehow, he got in and out unnoticed.

Around midnight Edwin finally wound down. I thought he'd leave until he said he had nowhere to go.

"My house is a crime scene and the cops won't let me in. All the motels in town are full of tourists here for that stupid Polka Daze. I don't have anywhere to go. This is your town, not mine."

Too Dead to Dance

I stood up about to tell him that it was his own fault that he didn't have any friends. He'd lived here for years. He didn't have many more friends in the city where he grew up. I was just too tired to argue. I got him a blanket and pillow. "You can sleep on the sofa tonight. Find a place to go tomorrow night. And you'll have to be out of here by seven in the morning. I have an appointment."

"Fine. Fine," he mumbled, stretching out on the sofa, turning his back to me. Edwin never did understand the concept of an attitude of gratitude.

After locking the door to my bedroom, I noticed the bags from the Christmas Shop. I was about to stash them on a shelf in my closet when I remembered the pickle ornament. My curiosity got the best of me and I opened the box and read the "Story of the Pickle Ornament."

It turns out that this German tradition is actually a legend about German immigrant, John Lower. "The Christmas Pickle" appears to have had its beginning right here in the good old U. S.A.

The story goes that John Lower was born in Bavaria in 1842. He left Germany with his family and immigrated to the United States. While fighting in the American Civil War, John Lower was captured and sent to a prison in Andersonville, Georgia. He soon fell ill given the poor conditions of the prison.

Starving, he begged of a guard for just one pickle before resigning to his death. The guard took pity on him, found and gave John Lower a pickle. Lower family lore declares that the pickle gave him the mental and physical strength to live on. After being reunited with his family, he began the tradition of hiding a pickle on the Christmas tree. The first person who found the pickle on Christmas morning would be blessed with a year of good fortune... and a special gift, just as John Lower had experienced!

What a nice story, I thought as I donned my

Sponge Bob sleep shirt, took two more pills, and crawled into bed. No Decker fantasies tonight. Not with Edwin in the next room. Besides, I had a headache.

I woke up in the middle of the night by shadowy figure standing at the foot of my bed calling my name and shaking my foot. I heard him crunching a piece of paper, opening it up and crunching it again, over and over. Then he called my name.

"Jennie, get up. Get up now!"

I sat up in bed, still half asleep. Edwin hovered at the foot of the bed shaking my ankle. "Don't call me Jennie," I said, still groggy and wondering why he was crackling paper.

"Jennie, the house is on fire. We have to get out of here!"

Confused, I got up, grabbed my cotton housecoat and donned a pair of slippers.

"How did you get in here? I locked the door."

"Never mind. We need to get out. The house is on fire. Damn it, Jennie, move!"

When I heard sirens coming closer, my brain finally kicked in and I followed Edwin out of the bedroom toward the back door. I hit the button to open the garage door, which slid open effortlessly. We ran through the garage and out into the night, brightly lit by the flames coming from the front of my house.

I ran down the driveway then glanced behind me at the facade of my townhouse. The row of shrubs lining the front of the structure danced in the blaze. Soon the attached houses on each side would be flare up as well.

The fire truck pulled up and suddenly the place swarmed with people in slick yellow coats unwinding hoses and spraying water on my house. A firefighter ran over to us. "Are you alright? Is anyone else in the house?"

We assured him we were fine and the only people in the house. "What about the people on each side of my house? Are they okay?"

He pointed toward the street and replied,

"Everyone is fine. Please step across the street, behind the truck so you don't get hurt."

My slippers slapped against my heels as I followed Edwin across the street. I glanced up to see Megan waving to me from the curb. I ran over and threw myself into her arms. I began to shake, aware of the danger I had eluded.

"My God, Jennifer. Who started your house on fire?" A squad car pulled up near us and Detective Decker lunged out of the car and ran over to me. Grabbing my arm, he twirled me around and enveloped me in his muscular arms. "Are you okay? Are you hurt? Who started the fire?"

I let him hold me for a few moments while I assured him I hadn't been hurt. When he let me go, Edwin moved up next to me, a haughty leer on his face. "Jennie, aren't you going to introduce me to your friend?"

I opened my mouth to tell him to mind his own business, when lightning flashed, and thunder crashed and the skies opened up. In seconds, we were drenched and so was the fire.

Megan yelled to us to follow her and we ran to her front porch. Her farmhouse style home with its long front porch, the width of the house, accommodated a wooden glider, several chairs, and a round wicker table. I was on the second step when Detective Decker grabbed my hand to stop me. "I see you're busy. I have to go. I just wanted to make sure you were okay. I'll talk to you later."

Before I could say anything, he crossed the street, got into his car, maneuvered around the firefighters' equipment, and turned the corner. What the hell had just happened? I glanced at Megan who nodded her head and rolled her eyes toward Edwin. I looked back at him; I shouldn't have been surprised at the nasty sneer on his face.

"For a guy with no place to sleep, you shouldn't look so smug," I said, mad enough to spit.

"Oh, who cares? As soon as the fire trucks get out of my way, I'll drive over to Glencoe and sleep in my office."

Megan stepped in front of him. "Edwin Heinz, get off my porch."

"It's still raining," he protested.

"Who cares?" Megan and I said in unison. Sometimes great minds do think alike.

Edwin pulled up his collar, stuck his hands in his pants pockets, and moseyed down the steps and across the street.

"How could you stay married to that ass for so many years?"

"I plead insanity. I think I just found out what the urge to kill truly means. Can I crash on your couch after I get done talking to the firefighters?"

"Well, ma'am," the firefighter said, "We found this glass in the bushes. It looks like someone threw a beer bottle filled with gas at your house and started it on fire."

"A Molotov cocktail? Who would do a thing like that?" I glanced at the bottle and recognized the label—Leinenkugel.

All of a sudden, Detective Decker walked in to the lighted area and stepped around the fireman, "Someone who wants you to stop nosing around. This is where you step back, Jennifer. It's too dangerous for you to keep snooping. Your hubby and I can't be around all the time to protect you."

"He's not my hubby and he wasn't protecting me. He was just being his normal obnoxious self. Where did you come from? I thought you left."

"I did but when Edwin's car passed me going ten miles over the speed limit I had to make a choice; either pull him over and give him a ticket or come back here and be with you."

My throat closed up and I willed myself not to cry. "I'm too tired to deal with this tonight. I'll come in to the Sheriff's Department in the morning with Sister

Bernadine. I suppose you think she tried to burn down my house, too."

I turned and slowly climbed the stairs to Megan's porch. We walked in and when she turned off the porch light, I looked out the little window in the door. Detective Decker was still standing there. He stuck his hands in his pockets and turned away. I bit my tongue to keep from calling him back while I watched him get into his truck and slowly drive away.

When the firemen put away their equipment and the truck drove down the street, Megan and I took a quick tour of my townhouse. Nothing seemed to be amiss but the place smelled acrid and smoky. My foam neck brace was lying on the floor next to the bed. I must have taken it off in my sleep. My neck felt okay, so I left it there and grabbed some dry clothes. We opened a few windows and turned on exhaust fans in the bathroom and kitchen, then locked up.

Back at Megan's, she pulled out the sofa bed for me and I gladly collapsed on it. Asleep before she switched off the light, this night had finally ended.

20

Monday

Megan shook me awake in what seemed like two minutes after I fell asleep. "Jennifer, get up. You promised Bernie you'd go with her to see Jacobs and Decker."

I dragged my tired body into the shower. It woke me up but I still felt as if my limbs were made of stone. I dressed and was digging my keys out of my purse when Megan handed me a fried egg sandwich on toast. "Eat this on your way. Here's a cup of coffee. Go!" She stuck a thermo cup in my hand and pushed me out the door.

I crossed the street, pushing the remote on my keychain. My garage door shrieked open in jerks and starts. What the heck was wrong with that door? I'd have to check it later; I had to get to the Sheriff's Office. I took a bite of the sandwich and gulped down some coffee before I backed out and down my driveway.

I met Bernie on the steps to the station house. We had arrived at practically the same time. I told her the condensed version of last night's excitement. "Unless they can prove you were the one who tried to burn my house down last night, you should be off the hook, Bernie."

"From your mouth to God's ears, Jennifer. Father Werner had me in his office last night. I thought he'd blow a gasket but remarkably, he seemed understanding. He knows I'd never hurt another human being and he even said he'd come with me today if I wanted him to. Just knowing he is standing by me is enough."

We went in the front door this time. Walking up to the glass-fronted window I was about to tell the perky young blonde receptionist that we were here to see Lt. Jacobs when she looked up and exclaimed, "Sister Bernadine! How are you?"

Bernie smiled. "I've been better. How are you, Angelia? And how's your mother?"

"She's much better, Sister. Thanks for helping us get her into the nursing home. They take really good care of her there."

"I knew they would. Is she making friends?"

"Oh, heavens, yes. One of us kids visits her almost every day and sometimes I think we're intruding. The other day I came right when bingo started and she made me go with her so she wouldn't miss it. Thank you so much for talking to her and making her realize it was best for her to be there."

"I was glad to help, Angelia. We're here to see Lieutenant Jacobs. Is her around?"

"I'll let him know that you're here. You can sit and wait over there," she said, pointing to two cushioned benches against the wall. She picked up the phone. This was worse than the waiting room at the dentist's office. I hoped Jacobs would call us soon.

A few minutes later Jacobs ambled through the door. "Good morning, ladies. Thanks for coming in." He waved his arm with a flourish showing us the door he wanted us to go through.

We were ushered to that same small grey room. This time it smelled like urine. I wondered who was here before us.

"Well, Sister, looks like there's been some excitement since I last talked to you." Looking at me he said, "Are you alright Jennifer?"

When I assured him I was fine and the damage to my house was only minimal, he turned again to Bernie.

"Okay, Sister, let's go over everything again."

Bernie told the whole story again with Lieutenant Jacobs asking questions and helping her to be more specific on a number of points. It took over two hours but finally Jacobs decided he'd learned everything Bernie was willing to tell him. He appeared to believe her when Bernie said Marty had been alive when she left her. He noted time lines and made other notations in his little notebook.

Before we left, I asked Jacobs, "Did you check out Bobby and where he was Thursday night?"

"Yes, Jennifer. I'm afraid that Sally lied to you. Bobby was at her house."

"Maybe she just said that to get him off the hook." "Sorry. We checked with the neighbors and his Camaro was in her driveway until Sunday morning."

I shook my head. "I'm glad he's not the killer, but I'm so disappointed that Sally lied to me."

Bernie looked at me and crossed her arms over her chest. "She probably lied because it was none of your business."

"Bernie, I was trying to help you."

"I know, but in the process you stuck your nose in where you had no business and you snuck into my office to retrieve information that I had kept in confidence for years."

Jacobs and I both looked at her open-mouthed. I asked, "How did you know?"

"One of the ushers at Mass saw you coming up from downstairs. He thought you had been down there to see me. It didn't take much to figure out what you'd been up to. I'm very disappointed in you, Jennifer."

"Oh, God, I'm sorry, Bernie. I just wanted to help."

"I know and it's the only reason that I'm still talking to you, but the Lieutenant is right. You need to butt out and let the police do their job."

"Thank you very much, Sister Bernadine," Jacobs

said. "I couldn't have said it better myself."

Totally embarrassed, I stood up to leave. Jacobs held up a hand. "Wait a minute, Jennifer. Just what were you looking for and what did you find in Sr. Bernadine's office?"

"That's confidential, Lieutenant Jacobs," Bernie said. "It was none of Jennifer's business and it's none of yours."

"Does this information relate to this case or anyone involved in it?"

Bernie stood up next to me. "I can assure you, Lieutenant Jacobs, that Jennifer found no pertinent information that you are not already aware of."

She bowed her veiled head toward him then turned and walked out of the room. I followed her but not before I saw Jacobs break out in a huge grin.

Along with being mortified at being "outed" by my friend in front of the police, I was disappointed to note that Detective Decker hadn't shown up. I thought I might have a chance to explain to him what Edwin had been doing at my house last night.

Then I mentally slapped myself. I didn't owe Decker any explanations. Who did he think he was to be upset by anything I did? I mentally jumped on my high horse and rode off into the sunset.

Jacobs accompanied us to the front desk. Bernie pulled opened the door and Detective Decker walked in. I melted. He was so darn cute.

I was so tuned in to Detective Decker that I didn't notice that someone was with him. Trailing behind him, head bowed was my about-to-be-ex-husband. How nice.

"Edwin, what are you doing here?"

"Ask your friend here. He thinks I killed Marty and started the fire at your place last night."

Detective Decker turned and put his hands on his hips. "As a matter of fact, Mr. Heinz, I asked you to come in and talk to us about the events you witnessed yesterday. You have to admit, you're in the middle of two serious incidents."

"Talk to my wife here. She's been at the same places I have."

I jumped into the fray. "I beg your pardon. Do you honestly think I set my own house on fire? And don't call me your wife."

"Who knows what you might do? You've been a little crazy lately."

"Not so crazy that you didn't come running to me when you need a place to sleep. And how did you get into my room last night? I know I locked that door."

Edwin flashed me a nasty grin before he turned away from me and spoke to Detective Decker. "Let's get this over with. I have things to do."

Detective Decker nodded his head, and took Edwin by the arm. They turned and walked through the door marked, "No Admittance" that we had just left. I was glad the room smelled of urine. It would annoy Edwin and, if I was lucky, might even start aggravating his allergies. I grabbed Bernie's hand and ambled out the door.

Bernie and I stopped for quick burgers at Chick's Drive-In. While sitting in the car munching on fries, I told Bernie about the conversation Megan and I had with Lisa Vetter earlier in the day.

"What were you doing at the Fest Grounds after everyone else left?" I asked.

"Oh, good Lord. Thank goodness you didn't mention that while we were at the Sheriff's Office. Jacobs would have put me in a cell."

"So, what were you doing there?"

"Why do you think it's any of your business, Jennifer? Have you forgotten already that you promised Jacobs to butt out of his investigation?"

"I didn't promise anyone anything. I just listened to you two berate me for trying to keep you out of jail!"

"You're right." Bernie's shoulder's sagged and she looked me right in the eye.

"I was looking for Natalie Younger."

"Natalie? What on earth did you want with her?"

"She called me. She was a little drunk and got melancholy. I found her and drove her home. She was crying about being single. She took care of her sick mother for years, you know. She's a very lonely woman, Jennifer. She never had a husband or children and now she feels that life has passed her by."

"I never thought of her that way, Bernie. I just think of her as a gossipy pain in the rear."

"She's feeling desperate, Jennifer. She wants what she thinks is a normal life. I've been telling her for years that there are other worthy routes for women to take besides marriage and family. Her job at the newspaper office isn't fulfilling for her, although I've never met anyone who can proofread better than her."

"So, what advice did you give her?"

"None. You can't reason with someone who's drunk. I just took her home and made her promise to call me later."

"Did she?" I asked.

"No. And she probably won't until she's feeling desperate again. I probably should call her but this has been going on for years. I keep trying to get her to go back to school and finish her degree, but she's afraid. I think that maybe she's comfortable in her rut. Or perhaps she still thinks that her white knight will ride in and take her away from it all."

"Wow! I never knew."

"And you don't know now, Jennifer." Bernie began wagging her finger at me again. "You keep your mouth shut about this and about Sally. Just because you know things doesn't mean you have to tell anyone. Not even Megan."

"But Megan wouldn't tell anyone—"

"It doesn't matter. You just keep this to yourself."
"Okay," I replied. "My lips are sealed."

I dropped off Bernie at the church and decided to check out Oma's Attic for the beer stein. I pulled into the parking lot in front of the second-hand store.

The building looked like it was previously a fish and chips franchise. A new coat of red and white paint spruced it up. I walked up the ramp and opened the door, expecting to see clothing and Christmas ornaments. What a surprise. Three neat bookcases held second hand books of all kinds, sorted by fiction and non-fiction then shelved by author's last name. I picked up a couple Denise Swanson mysteries that I hadn't yet read.

The rest of the store held glass topped counters with a variety of objects in them. Each case had its own theme. One held jewelry. Another held glass figurines. I found a case that appeared to hold things with a German theme. There were clear glass beer mugs, German flags, a nutcracker, several hand-blown glass Christmas ornaments.

A teenage girl bounced up to me and said, "Can I help you?"

"Yes, I'm looking for a beer stein. Do you have any?" "Gee, I don't know. What's a beer stein?"

Oh, boy. "It's a mug with a lid and it usually has some sort of scene on it. Here let me show you a picture of the one I'm looking for."

"Sure, fine," she replied, checking out the chipped polish on her nails.

I pulled the picture that Laura had emailed me from my purse. "Do you have anything like this here?"

"Naw, I don't think so. Look around if you want."

I was surprised to find the sales clerk so uninterested when it was clear that someone cared a great deal about the display of the items for sale in the store.

"Who is Oma?" I asked.

"She's my aunt. She had a doctor's appointment today and my mom made me work here until she gets back."

"Until who gets back? Your aunt or your mother?"

"My aunt. What difference does it make? Do you want to look around or not?"

"Not," I said, setting the books down as I turned to walk out.

Just as I reached out my hand to open the door, it opened. I gave a surprised little yelp.

The woman who walked through the door wore her silver-white hair in a short bob. She reached out her hand and touched my arm. "I'm sorry. I didn't mean to startle you."

"That's okay I said, moving around her to go through the door.

"Did you find what you were looking for?"

I looked at her and frowned. Why should she care, I thought?

She must have realized what I was thinking. "This is my shop. Can I help you?"

"You're Oma?" Except for the hair color, she looked too young to be a grandmother.

"Well, I'm somebody's Oma. I have three grandchildren. Yes, this is my store. What can I help you find?" She shoved her purse under the counter and looked at me expectantly.

"Here's a picture of the beer stein I'm looking for." "Isn't that lovely. I wish I had this stein here," she said, handing the picture back to me. "It would sell in a minute. No, I don't have any steins here right now. I sold three of them last week, right before Polka Daze. I always sell a lot of German items this time of year."

I picked up the paperback books I had abandoned and said, "I'll take these."

When I paid for my purchases, I gave her my card and asked her to call me if she came across the stein. She walked with me across the store and as she opened the door for me she said, "I'm sorry I wasn't here when you came. My niece isn't very good at this but she was the only person I could find on short notice."

"She said you were at the doctor's office. Are you okay?"

"Oh, I'm fine. Just had to get a couple shots. My husband and I are going to Israel next week."

"What a delightful reason to go to the doctor. Well, not the shots but a trip to Israel! I hope you have a fantastic vacation."

"Oh, thank you. I'm sure we will."

I walked back to my car with my purse swinging at my side. Israel! What a great place to visit. I had to put that on my "to-do-before-I-die" list. I tossed my purse on the seat and began to back out of my space when I glimpsed into the rearview mirror and saw movement.

I stomped on the brakes and watched my purse fly off the seat and roll under the dash. I jumped out and ran to the back of the car. There I found a run-away shopping cart from the hardware store next to Oma's. The wind must have blown it across the parking lot. I moved it out of the way, got back in my car, and drove home. I forgot about my purse until I pulled into my garage. When I looked down, I saw the contents spilled all over the floor mat. I scooped everything up and just dumped back into my purse.

When I walked through the kitchen door, I noticed that smoky smell was mostly gone so I turned off the exhaust fans. Grabbing a basket, I threw some clothes in it and headed to the laundry room.

Tossing my smoke smelling laundry into the washer, I pulled off my sweater and threw it in with the other clothes—it had a pickle stain on the front. I picked up the shirt I had worn the night Wes was killed. It needed more than detergent.

Aiming the nozzle of the stain remover at my shirt, I pressed the button. The can sputtered and spit out a little glob of foam. Impatiently, I trudged to the kitchen and looked under the sink for a new can.

The bright red can should've been easy to spot, but I couldn't find it among the other spray cans there. I got down on my knees and reached to the back of the cabinet, knocking over a few cans.

Too Dead to Dance

Impatiently, I began pulling everything out of the cupboard. I found the ant killer, window cleaner, scrubbing bubbles, and finally the stain remover. Why hadn't I seen it in there?

Déjà vu, all over again, to quote Yogi Berra. The red spray can. The red carabineer in Sister Bernadine's office. The red knitting needle in Wes' neck. Red looks black in the dark. A red cargo truck. Bingo!

I pulled the pickle-stained sweater back over my head and dug in my purse for my cell phone. It wasn't there. I dumped the purse out on the kitchen table. It definitely wasn't there. The car! It was probably on the floor where my purse landed. I ran out to the garage and opened the passenger door. Nothing on the floor. I reached under the seat and grabbed something. When I pulled it out I saw that it was my checkbook. Where was my phone? Then I spotted my little navy blue phone tucked into the cup holder. I flipped it open and called the Sheriff's Office as I walked back into the kitchen.

Angelia answered the phone. When I asked for Jacobs, she said, "He's not in right now. May I take a message?"

"Angelia, this is Jennifer Penny, Sister Bernadine's friend. Do you know where I can find him or Detective Decker?"

"Oh, hi, Ms. Penny. You know, I think Detective Decker said something to someone on his way out that he was going to the Fest Grounds. Although, I don't know why. Polka Daze is over."

I thanked her, and was about to hang up when she asked, "Do you want me to have either one of them to call you?"

"No, Angelia, but if you talk to them could you tell them that I went to the Fest Grounds?"

"Sure thing, Ms. Penny."

I hung up and started shoving things from the kitchen table back into my purse. Then I stuck my cell phone in my pocket and took off for the Fest Grounds.

Cars and trucks were arriving and leaving the

Fest Grounds when I arrived. Cars were now parked where just the day before food stands had sent out delicious aromas. I pulled up and parked right in front of the Home Arts Building.

When I stuck my head in, I saw a few vendors packing up their wares. They talked in hushed tones in this almost empty building. It was so unlike the hustle and bustle of the previous weekend. My coffee booth was completely gone. My efficient employees had arrived early and moved everything back to the warehouse to await the next festival or event.

Turning, I walked through the grounds. The smallest tent was rolled up. It took six men to pick it up and put it on a flatbed truck. The medium sized tent was down and several men stood around looking at it. Maybe they were waiting for it to do something.

I looked for Decker's truck then realized he and Jacobs were probably in a squad car. I didn't see any of those either. If they were in an unmarked car, I wouldn't recognize it. I had again run off without thinking things through and now I didn't know what to do. I continued to walk through the grounds looking for Decker or Jacobs. Jacobs would stand out if he were here because he always wore a suit and the men here wore work clothes.

When I came to the largest tent, I saw a dozen men pulling on ropes attached to it. Someone was shouting orders. I watched as the huge canvas structure billowed in the wind, and then sank to the ground like a balloon losing air. The men gave a cheer when it settled like a huge white puddle.

When I turned to check out the Christmas Shop, the big double doors were both open and the red cargo truck from Metzger's Meat Market was backed up and blocking one side of the entryway. Cautiously entering through the doublewide barn doors, my steps echoed through the small building. It no longer looked like a fairyland. The cement block walls were cracked. The cold cement floor completed the bleakness, so different from the magical Christmas Shop.

Folded tables were lined up along one side of the room. Someone was stacking chairs against the other wall. I peeked into the back of the cargo truck and saw more folding chairs.

When the man stacking chairs turned, I saw that it was the Fest Meister. "Frank! What are you doing here?" I realized I was relieved that it was Frank and not Al.

"Hi, Ms. Penny. I'm just stacking the chairs from the small tent. This is where we store them."

"I'm just surprised to see you with the truck. I thought that Al was the only one who used it."

Frank smiled and took the toothpick from his mouth. "It seems that way to me sometimes, too. He sure likes this truck, but I use it occasionally. Can I help you with something?"

"Maybe. Frank, I think Al may be in trouble."
"What kind of trouble?"

"I think he may have tried to run me off the road the other night."

"Why would he want to do that? Did you see the driver?"

"Not then, Frank, but I saw Al driving the truck as I left the Fest Grounds. One of the Princesses was sitting next to him. At first I thought the truck was a black or dark blue SUV, but I just figured out that red looks black in the night."

"Why would my brother want to run you off the road?" Frank asked again.

"I'm not sure. I think Al may have gotten into it with Wes. I'm so sorry, Frank, but I think Al was involved in that bank robbery a few years ago. I think he needed the money for his portion of the meat market that he bought with you."

"Aw, what are you talking about? Are you nuts? Al had a good job. He saved that money for his share and he invested it wisely."

"Maybe you don't know your brother as well as

you think you do. People aren't always as they appear."

"No they aren't, Missy. Why did you have to stick your nose into other people's business?" Frank flashed a scornful grin that frightened me. Suddenly this sweet little man looked intimidating. Something flashed as he pulled his hand out of his pocket. By the time I realized what he was doing, he had flipped open a menacing knife with a needle sharp point. Snatching my arm, he pulled me closer. I felt my whole body grow cold. "Oh, crap, it wasn't Al, it was you," I whispered.

Why didn't I realize that the pudgy little man who seemed to be everywhere at Polka Fest wouldn't be missed for short periods. People would just think he was at a different tent on the Fest Grounds. And the red truck with the sausage man on the side was so familiar around town, that no one would pay any attention to it parked on a residential street.

"You should learn to mind your own business, girlie. I tried to warn you. Now I'm going to have to shut you up, too. I've got nothing to lose at this point."

Stall, I had to stall, I thought. I put my hand in my sweater pocket and pushed the number 4 button, then the "send" button on the phone. At least I hoped that I had pushed the right buttons. "I understand why you killed Wes. He wanted his share of the money from the bank robbery, didn't he? You spent it all to buy your share of the meat market."

"Damned economy. I would've had the money to pay Wes if my stocks hadn't tanked. I just didn't have the money to give him. I tried to explain, but he wouldn't listen. When he hit me in the stomach, I just grabbed the first thing I saw and stuck him. I just wanted him to stop hurting me. I didn't mean to kill him."

I took a little step forward, moving in real close to him, hoping he'd automatically move back. It worked but he was still a good way away from the door. There were people all over the fairgrounds. If I could get close to the door, I could yell and maybe someone would hear me and come to help.

"I heard that you saved money for years to buy the meat market. Why did you need to rob the bank?" Another tiny step forward.

"It was my wife. It's all her fault."

"Why? Did her illness take all your savings?" One more step.

"No, we had insurance for that. She gambled it all away. While I was working to save for our future, she was at the casino losing it faster than I could earn it. The cancer finally slowed her down, but by then she'd lost all of our savings."

"I heard that you used her life insurance to buy your share." Another step. We were getting closer to the door but not close enough for me to be sure someone would hear me if I yelled.

"Ha! I only had a $10,000 policy on her. The funeral took most of that. I was desperate. I had no other choice."

"What about Marty? Why kill her?" I asked.

The Fest Meister shook his head and waved the knife around. "Man, she wouldn't shut up. She demanded I give her Wes' share. Kept telling me she'd blow the whistle on me. Stupid broad. All Wes did was drive the car. And he almost took off without me when the shooting started. Why should that broad get anything? I thought I'd just get in and out of her house while her stupid boyfriend was at church. Then you women stared coming in and out of the house. I almost got caught when her boyfriend walked in the front door just as I slipped out the back way. Now we're done talking."

He grabbed my arm, and pushed me in front of him, toward the back of his truck.

Poking the knife at me, I jumped as he said, "Move! I took a few steps forward, then spun around, put both hands on his chest, and pushed with all my might. Frank fell backwards and crashed into a stack of folding chairs. The chairs fell off the rack and Frank hit the floor. I turned and ran through the door, shouting and waving my arms. A hand reached out and grabbed my arm. I screamed. Detective Decker pulled me into his arms as Jacobs moved into the doorway pointing a gun at the Fest Meister.

"Drop the knife, Metzger. It's all over." Jacobs said. "You tricked me! You can't do this to me. I'm the Fest Meister!" He leaned over and placed his hunting knife on the cement floor.

Jacobs gave him an amused grin. "Fest Meister, you have the right to remain silent . . ."

I looked around and saw four squad cars along with the black sedan that I realized was Jacobs and Decker's unmarked car.

Lieutenant Jacobs put the Fest Meister in the back of one of the squad cars and they left the Fest Grounds.

Decker grabbed me by the shoulders. "That was an incredibly stupid thing to do, Jennifer. You could've been hurt."

"Didn't Angelia tell you where I was?"

"Yes, but what if we hadn't checked in?" "Did you get my cell phone call?"

"Yes, it's the reason we knew you were in trouble." "See, I knew you'd show up," I bluffed.

"What if we had been on the other side of the county? Jennifer, you could've been killed, damn it."

Whoops, I hadn't thought of that.

Just as I was searching for an answer, Decker pulled me into a bear hug and kissed me. Believe me it was worth waiting for.

I closed the front door and leaned against it. What a day. Suddenly, my knees were weak and I could barely stand up. My God! I could have been killed! I needed a drink. No wine cooler tonight. I grabbed the bottle of rum and poured a big dollop into a water glass. I added some ice and a little Coke and took a big swallow.

The drink calmed me down but suddenly I was

exhausted. I looked at my big empty bed and donned a pair of pajamas, grabbed a pillow and afghan and headed for the sofa.

Diane Morlan

21

Tuesday

  I pushed the "end" button on my cell phone and stuck it in my purse. Snatching my car keys off the table, I rushed out the door into the garage. Megan and Bernie would be here to pick me up in a half hour and I needed to check out the last store for Laura's Coke stein. One more place to check and then I'd be done with this exasperating beer stein quest.
  I found a parking place right in front of 422 Center Street, right in the middle of the downtown area. This is where the "Coins to Cups" store was supposed to be. However, the script on the window announced "Messer's Jewelry." I looked at the paper in my hand. It read 422. I looked around to the stores next to and across the street from the jewelry store. Ben Franklin, Aunt Martha's Confectionery, Book Nook. No coin shop.
  I got out of my car and walked toward the jewelry store. Thinking that Coins to Cups might have gone out of business, I decided to ask at the jewelry store if they knew anything about the previous owner. When I got to the door, I saw under the large gold script declaring Messer's Jewelry a smaller sign--Coins to Cups.
  I went inside and walked past glass show cases

sparsely filled with jewelry. About a dozen wristwatches and pocket watches were in the first case. Bracelets and earrings were in the second. The type of stones sorted them. There were gold chains and bracelets.

Across from them were cases that held rings. A considerable number of diamond engagement and wedding rings along with ruby, emerald, and pearl rings arranged much the same as the other jewelry.

As I perused the contents of each showcase, I heard a snapping, popping noise coming from the back of the store. I made my way toward the sound and saw a woman sitting behind the counter, snapping the gum she was intently chewing.

Her head was down and she was poised over something on her desk with an odd little tool in her hand. When I got up to the counter I saw that she had the back of a man's watch open and was using the tool to poke at something in the watch.

She looked up and appeared surprised to see me standing there. "Oh, hi. I didn't hear you come in. The buzzer must not be working. Can I help you?"

"Yes, I'm looking for Coins to Cups. This is the address I have for it."

"Yeah, it's in the back." She pointed her thumb over her shoulder. I looked where she had pointed and saw a glass door with a sign bearing the same gold script as the one on the front door. "Thanks," I said, walking toward the back door.

The woman answered, "No problem." She had already dismissed me and was back to poking at the watch and snapping her gum.

When I opened the door to Coins to Cups, jingle bells attached to the inside door handle announced me. The room was wide but very short. Only about eight feet separated me from the woman standing behind the counter. Young and perky, she beamed at me. "Welcome, come in and look around. Let me know if I can be of help to you."

"Thanks," I replied, looking around the

minuscule shop.

There were two other people in the shop, both older men leaning over a table where the perused several coins laid out in front of them.

Instead of showcases, the coins were in loose-leaf books stacked on the table where the two men were standing, paging through them. Each black binder had information on the spine—country, denomination, and year they were minted.

Three rows of narrow wooden shelves surrounded the room. The shelves held cups, mugs, steins and other drinking vessels. There didn't seem to be any rhyme or reason to the display. It appeared that when one cup was purchased, another took its place, regardless of color, size or anything else.

I turned toward the sprightly sales clerk and said, "I've never been in a store within a store before."

"Everyone asks about the store the first time the come here. My Dad owns the building. When my sister took over the jewelry store when he retired, he had this part sectioned off for me because he knew how much I wanted a coin shop."

"That was so thoughtful. Is it working out for you?" "I'll say! I've been here three years now and it's doing quite well."

I'd have liked to talk to her longer but I needed to complete my task. "Do you have any Coca-Cola beer steins?" I figured it would take less time to ask than to check each cup on each shelf. Besides, it seemed on this beer stein hunt, the more I looked, the more I bought.

"Absolutely!" she answered, coming around the counter and pointing to the wall to my right while moving toward it. Here's one. It's really cute." She lifted a Santa mug off the shelf. She was right, it was cute. Santa sat with a Coke glass in his hand while an elf dressed in green poured Coke from a bottle into the glass. The handle of the mug was shaped like a Coke bottle. "This is very cute," I told her, "but it's not what I'm looking for. Here's a picture of the one I need."

Too Dead to Dance

She took the picture from my hand and with her index finger on her mouth, she pondered. "You know, I've seen this beer stein."

"You have? Did you sell it?"

"No. I didn't have it, but I saw it."

Oh, joy! I was getting closer. "Where did you see it" "I don't know. I can't remember. I was going to buy it but I was in a hurry and thought I'd go back later. Then I forgot all about it until now. Where did I see it?"

I waited, hoping she would remember.

"Nope, can't remember." She said, holding out the picture.

"Can I leave my number with you? If you come across it or remember where you saw it, would you call me? I'd truly love to buy it."

"Sure, I can do that."

I handed her my card and mentally crossed the last name off my list.

Before I left, I looked at the men paging through the coin books. "Hey, Randy. I didn't know you were a coin collector."

Bernie's old beau, Randy Vetter turned and greeted me. "Hi, Jennifer. I just collect pennies. Been doing it since fifth grade. Remember Mrs. Huber? She got me started."

"I loved Mrs. Huber. She was like a chubby aunt. Randy, I'm sorry the police bothered you."

"They didn't really bother me, Jennifer," Randy said, shrugging his shoulders. "They bothered Lisa though. I was just surprised when they showed up at my door."

"I hope Lisa isn't still mad at me."

"She'll get over it now that they arrested Frank. She sure was in a snit wasn't she?" Randy laughed and stuck a toothpick in his mouth. "She's one fiery woman." He patted me on the shoulder. "Take care, Jennifer." Turning to the girl behind the counter, he asked, "Got any of those new Lincoln pennies? I need the one with the log cabin on the back."

Bernie and Megan were waiting in my driveway when I pulled up. I parked the car in the garage and listened once again as the door creaked close. I really had to call someone about that.

"Where have you been?" Megan called to me from her open window.

I jumped into the back seat of Megan's SUV and said, "Let's go, girls. I'm hungry for potato pancakes."

Megan pulled out and we were on our way to have breakfast at our favorite place.

While we stuffed ourselves with pancakes, bacon, eggs, and toast, we discussed the events of the day before.

The waitress at Dottie's Diner, whose nametag read "Pansy" took the empty plates off the table and said, "I'll bring the coffee pot over, looks like you're going to be here for a while."

"Is the manager in?" I asked. "I'd like to talk to him if he is."

"Did I do something wrong?" Pansy asked.

"Oh, no. Of course not. I have a business proposition for him." "He doesn't come in today until three. Can I help you?"

"As a matter of fact you can," I said, pulling a three-pound bag of my best restaurant blend from my oversized purse. "Have him try this out and then give me a call. I can give him a very good price if he likes my product."

It was almost lunchtime and we were still hashing over the events of the last few days. Megan set her coffee mug on the table. "The best part was when I kicked Edwin off my porch while it was raining. He actually sputtered."

Pansy had just brought a coffee carafe to our table and began refilling our cups when Detective Decker slid into the booth next to me. "I thought I'd find you here," he said to me. He casually lifted his arm and rested it across the back of the booth with his fingers just barely touching my shoulder.

Too Dead to Dance

"How did you find us?" I asked. This was our secret place.

"I'm a detective, remember?" He smiled that wicked smiled at me.

"Yeah, great job detecting the Fest Meister, Mister." Had I really said that?

"We would've gotten there, Jennifer, and without putting anyone in danger."

Crossing my arms, I sat up straighter in the booth. "Listen, Detective Decker…"

"You can call me Jerry, you know. We're not strangers anymore." Again with that smile. I may have even blushed, remembering that kiss.

Before I could think up a retort, Pansy plopped a cup in front of Decker and filled it from the carafe she'd left on the table. "Want your usual burger and fries, Jerry?" she asked.

Decker nodded, and then looked at me as if he'd just been caught with his hand in a cookie jar. "Great detecting, Jerry." I said. While Decker ate his lunch, we peppered him with questions.

The Fest Meister had saved for years to start his own business. A year before the meat market went up for sale he found that Ida had been withdrawing money faster than Frank was depositing it. She gambled it all away.

Frank started saving again, this time putting the money in an account that Ida couldn't touch. About four years ago, she was diagnosed with cancer and died a few months later. When the meat market came up for sale, he talked his brother, Al into going into business with him. Since Al was a butcher it appeared to be a good idea and he told Frank he could come up with half the money.

Frank didn't have near enough money to pay his share and the closing was in thirty days. That's when he contacted Wes and Sally's father and they put together the plan to rob the bank.

"Trudy told me he used Ida's life insurance

money to buy the meat market." I said.

"That's what everyone thought. Turns out Frank only had a $10,000 policy on her. That's barely enough to pay for a funeral."

"I don't understand," I said. "I saw Al and one of the Princesses in the cargo truck when I left the Fest Grounds Saturday night. How did Frank get the truck and run me off the road?"

Decker pointed a finger at me. "That's what happens when amateurs get involved in police business. Al gave the Princess, who is his niece, a ride home. She only lived a few blocks away. When he got back to the Fest Grounds, Frank took the truck and Al stayed around to dance and party after the closing ceremony."

"I don't understand. Why did Frank kill Marty?" Bernie asked.

"Marty had no idea it was Frank who had killed Wes. She demanded that he pay her the share he owed Wes. She knew all along that Wes was in on the bank robbery."

"She told us she didn't know anything about it," I said.

"Jennifer, people lie all the time. Did you expect her to tell you she was involved in the extortion attempt of a bank robber?"

Frank had parked his truck around the corner from her house, threaded his way through various backyards and came in Marty's back door. Marty thought he was there to pay her off.

When he left after killing her, he crossed a few different backyards and came out at his truck as if he'd just made a delivery. No one paid any attention to him since they were used to him or Al in the truck, driving all over town to deliver orders to homes and businesses. He had become invisible.

"Oh, good Lord," Bernie said, "What if he had come in while I was there?" She crossed herself.

"He saw you Sister," Decker told her. "He waited

for you to leave, then went in to confront Marty."

"What about Al?" Megan asked. "Was he involved at all?"

"No," Decker replied, "He thought, just like everyone else, that Frank had used his savings and Ida's life insurance to pay his share."

We were finishing our last cup of coffee when Natalie Younger trotted into the room.

"My, my, look who's here," she said, pulling a chair up to our booth and plopping down as close to Decker as she could get.

"Are you the new detective in town that I've been hearing so much about?" She actually, no kidding, batted her eyes at him.

While he was looking for an answer, I introduced him. "Detective Decker, meet Natalie Younger."

"Pleased to meet you, Miss Younger," he said, leaning away from her and closer to me. Under the table, he closed his hand around mine.

"What have you all been up to? I heard that you solved a murder, Jennifer. You certainly can get mixed up in the craziest things. Can't she Detective?"

Megan stood up. "Okay, gang, the bus is leaving." Since she'd driven, Bernie got up and I motioned to Decker to let me out.

Decker said, "Why don't I give you a ride home, Jennifer."

I readily agreed.

Natalie looked around and said, "You aren't all going to leave me here alone, are you? I haven't even ordered yet."

We all got up and Megan leaned over Natalie and said, "There are a couple of truckers up at the counter. Why don't you go sit up there and order your lunch?"

"What a great idea! Why, Megan, I didn't know you could be so nice." She got up and moseyed over to the counter.

When Natalie was out of sight, we all laughed aloud, except for Bernie.

"Shame on you, Megan. That was just naughty."

"I know, Bernie, but it sure was fun. Come on, we'll stop at the Dairy Queen on the way home."

"Oh, Megan. You say the nicest things." Bernie laughed and followed Megan to her SUV.

I turned to say goodbye to them when something caught my eye. I walked over to a shelf with a two-foot high sign in bright yellow with red letters spelling "Clearance."

I love a sale but that's not what I had seen. On the shelf beneath the sign was a red and green box with a Coca-Cola logo on it. I picked it up and shouted, "Whoopee. I found it!"

"Found what?" Jerry asked.

"I found the Coca-Cola Soda Fountain beer stein. I've been looking all over town for this little beauty."

"Why?"

I explained that a customer had seen it in town but couldn't remember where. "This place wasn't even on her list. I bet she came here for lunch and forgot all about it. No wonder she couldn't remember where she had seen it."

The biggest surprise was when I took it to the counter to pay for it. Clearance meant forty percent off. I found the beer stein and got a bargain to boot. Laura would be my customer forever! And the surf and turf dinner was mine!

We left the diner and Jerry helped me up into his truck. "Looks like I'm going to have to get a step-stool if we're going to be seeing each other."

I just looked at him, totally at a loss for words.

"I know you're skittish about getting into a relationship, Jennifer."

I started to deny it, then just shut up, for once and let Jerry finish.

"How about we start with that dinner date you promised me and see how it goes from there."

"Wait a minute," I said. "The deal was when you apologized to Bernie and me for suspecting her, I would go to dinner with you."

"I already apologized to Bernie. I went to church this morning and caught up with her after Mass. She graciously accepted my apology. And now, I sincerely apologize to you. I will never doubt you again. Your loyalty to your friends is amazing."

"If you think that's something, try messing with my kids," I said.

"Apology accepted?" He asked.

"Apology accepted," I replied.

By now, we were almost nose-to-nose. We were both smiling and I think my grin was probably as silly as his was.

Jerry started up the truck and eased out of the parking place. We crossed the river and headed across town to my townhouse.

"I'll pick you up about eight, okay?" Jerry asked. "Tonight?" I quickly computed how long I had to get ready.

"Yes, tonight. Do you have another date?"

"No. No. Of course not. Eight is fine. I'll be ready." I hope that was true. What was I going to wear? Did I have time to go shopping? It was three o'clock, no time to shop. I needed a facial.

I looked out the window just in time to see my favorite house, the Queen Anne with the whipped cream trim. "Stop!" I yelled, grabbing Decker's arm. He hit the brakes and we both careened forward.

"What?" He yelled.

"Look at that house," I said.

"What about it? Is it on fire or something?"

"No, not the big yellow house. The little blue one next to it."

"Yeah, what about it? I looks just like the big house only smaller."

"Yes. It's perfect. And it's for sale," I said, pointing to a River Valley Realtors sign in the front yard.

"Okay." Decker said, shaking his head and

motioning with his hand that I should say more.

"I've been thinking about moving out of the townhouse I live in. I need a place of my own. A real house, one with character. I think I may have found it." I dug in my purse for my cell phone and punched in the number on the sign.

The rooms were small, but not tiny. We peeked into each of the many windows. The turret provided the bedroom with a cozy niche, perfect for a comfy reading chair. There was even a one-car garage behind the house. It used the same driveway as the bigger house next door.

When we reached the back of the house, Jerry grabbed me up into his arms. He leaned down and brushed his lips across mine, then lingered there for a long soft kiss.

When we finally broke away, I felt dizzy. Then I peeked in a back window and saw a dining area at the back of the living room.

"Oh, my sideboard would fit in there. And there's room for the mirror, too."

The lovely little cottage was almost unnoticeable next to the huge Victorian, partly because it had been painted a dull slate blue. That was easily fixed. It looked like it was in good condition, even the roof looked new.

I called Megan on her cell and told her about the little house I had discovered.

"I'll check it out, Jennifer and get back to you. We should be able to see it tomorrow. It's not my listing so I want to check out what the asking price is and find out anything else that might be helpful."

I turned to Decker. "Do you like to paint?"

"No, but I could learn to like it." He picked up my hand and stroked it softly.

"Let's go peek in the windows. I can't wait to see the inside."

"Hey, I'm a cop. Do you want to get arrested as a peeping Tom?"

"Don't be silly," I chided. "No one's living there.

Too Dead to Dance

We can sneak a quick look."

I jumped out of the truck and Decker followed. I grabbed his hand and pulled him along behind me as I went from window to window all around the house.

"What's a sideboard?" Jerry asked.

"It's a beautiful piece of furniture that I'm going to put a down payment on tomorrow."

"That's nice," he said, putting his arm around me. "You do that." He nuzzled his lips against the back of my neck.

When Jerry finally pulled into my driveway, he asked, "Where would you like to go for dinner tonight?"

I looked into his gorgeous brown eyes and said, "Do you like Surf and Turf?"

MEGAN"S FAST AND EASY
ESPRESSO BROWNIES

Megan isn't exactly the domestic type, but she likes to putz around the kitchen. Try this somewhat homemade recipe and see for yourself.

Start with your favorite Brownie mix. Follow the instructions on package, substituting ¼ cup of espresso instead of the water.

After pouring brownie mix into the pan, sprinkle 2 - 3 Tbsp. crushed espresso beans over the top. Megan says you don't have to buy a whole package of espresso beans. She uses chocolate covered espresso beans.

Bake as indicated on the package.

Frosting.

Use ½ can of your favorite cake frosting. Add a shot of coffee liqueur and mix. Spread over cooled brownies.

TRUDY'S DOILY PATTERN

This is a great pattern for crocheters learning thread crochet.

Size: 8 ½" diameter.

Materials:
Crochet Cotton, 75 yds.
Crochet Hook:
Size Steel 7

Gauge: 1 rnd = 1" across

Rnd 1: Ch 8, sl st in first ch to form ring; ch 3 **(counts as first dc now and throughout)**, 23 dc in ring; join with sl st to first dc. (24 dc)

Rnd 2: Ch 6 (counts as dc, ch 3), (skip next st, dc in next st, ch 3) around; join with sl st to first dc. (12 dc)

Rnd 3: Ch 3, (5 dc in ch-3 sp, dc in next dc) around; join with sl st to first dc. (72 dc)

Rnd 4: Ch 3, 2 dc in same st as joining, (ch 5, skip 5 dc, 3 dc in next 3 dc) around; join with sl st to first dc. (36 dc)

Rnd 5: (Sl st, ch 1, sc) in next dc, (9 dc in next ch-5 sp, skip next dc, sc in next dc) around; join with sl st to first sc. (108 dc)

Rnd 6: Ch 6, (skip 2 sts, dc in next st, ch 3) around; join with sl st to first dc. (40 dc)

Rnd 7: Sl st in next ch-3 sp, ch 3, 4 dc in same sp, (ch 3, skip ch-3 sp, 5 dc in next ch-3 sp) around, ch 3; join with sl st to first dc. (100 dc)

Rnd 8: Sl st in next dc, (sl st, ch 3, 2 dc) in next dc, (ch 6, 3 dc in center dc of next 5-dc group) around, ch 6; join with sl st to first dc. (60 dc)

Rnd 9: (Sl st, ch 1, sc) in next dc, (11 dc in ch-6 sp, sc in center dc of next 3-dc group) around; join with sl st to first sc. (220 dc)

Rnd 10: Rep Rnd 6. (80 dc) Finish off and weave in ends.

Pattern by Maggie Weldon. **Maggie's Crochet** www.MaggiesCrochet.com

Diane Morlan was born in Aurora, Illinois in 1943. Diane likes to brag that she has had a library card since she was in Kindergarten.

When she was fifteen years old, her family moved to Minneapolis. Since then she has considered both Illinois and Minnesota her home state. In 1977, Diane earned a B.A. in Social Work at Minnesota State University

Moorhead. After working in that field for eight years, she returned to graduate school at the University of Minnesota where she earned an MSW. She worked as a psychotherapist at a community mental health center and a clinical social worker at a psychiatric hospital. Diane has also managed a group home for developmentally disabled adults. Moving away from the seriousness of social work, Diane worked for more than ten years managing a group of saleswomen, selling lingerie at home parties.

Like many people, Diane's dream was to write a novel someday. Currently she is semi-retired, works part-time at Kishwaukee College Library, and lives in Sycamore, IL. In 2007, Diane took a creative writing fiction course. One of the stories produced for that class won second prize and was published in the 2008 *Kameilian* Literary and Arts Magazine.

Diane has three children and six grandchildren. When not writing, she enjoys crocheting and visiting her friends in Minnesota. TOO DEAD TO DANCE is her first novel.

Watch for the second Jennifer Penny mystery, SHAKE DOWN DEAD.

NORMANDALE COMMUNITY COLLEGE
LIBRARY
9700 FRANCE AVENUE SOUTH
BLOOMINGTON, MN 55431-4399

CPSIA information can be obtained at www.ICGtesting.com
Printed in the USA
LVOW05s1226201113

362074LV00002B/327/P

9 781479 395248